JOHN LENNON SONGS

THIS IS A CARLTON BOOK

This edition published by Carlton Books Limited 1997

A CIP catalogue for this book is available from the British Library

ISBN 1-85868-352-1

Executive Editor: Lorraine Dickey
Editor: Ian Cranna
Art Direction: Zoë Maggs
Design: Sue Clarke
Picture Research: Charlotte Bush, Brenda Clynch
Production: Garry Lewis

Printed and bound in Dubai

The publishers would like to thank the following sources for their kind permission to reproduce the pictures in this book:

Archive Photos; Associated Press; Camera Press/Colman Doyle, Ben Ross; Corbis-Bettmann/UPI, Reuter; Hulton Getty; London Features International/Nick Elgar; Mary Evans Picture Library; Mirror Syndication International; Pictorial Press/Tony Gale, Polygram; Popperfoto; Redferns/Astrid Kirchhnerr, Michael Ochs Archive; Retna/Jak Kilby, Thomas Kristich, Michael Putland, Peter Smith; Rex Features/Henry T. Kaiser; S.I.N/Kieron Murphy; Starfile/Bob Gruen; Topham Picturepoint.

Every effort has been made to acknowledge correctly and contact the source and/or copyright holder of each picture, and Carlton Books Limited apologises for any unintentional errors or omissions which will be corrected in future editions of this book.

JOHN LENNON SONGS

The Stories Behind Every John Lennon Song 1970-1980

PAUL DU NOYER

CARLTON

CONTENTS

FOREWORD

There is really only one story behind John Lennon's songs — the story of his life. He once described songs as being like handwriting, because even a shopping list on a scrap of paper might reveal the personality of its creator. In the same way, music speaks to us about the person who wrote it. In Lennon's case that's doubly true — he approached his songs like they were the instalments of an autobiography. Each one opens a window on the man's inner self.

There are lots of books about John Lennon's life and the Beatles' music. What's often overlooked is the superb solo work that he produced in the final decade of his life. Between the end of the Beatles in 1970 and his terrible murder in 1980, Lennon kept on weaving dreams. Once he was free of the Beatles, his style became more confessional than ever. There is no finer way of reliving John Lennon's story than through this music.

I've loved Lennon's work for as long as I can remember. Perhaps you have, too. What follows are tales that may help you to enjoy it even more. As it happens, I wrote the book in Liverpool, London and New York, which is maybe the way that John would have wanted it. But I also know that he might have called it a load of crap. He'd be wrong, I hope, but John Lennon never specialised in being right — only in being magnificent.

We'd know far less of Lennon's life if it were not for the interviews he gave just before his death, when he was promoting his last album *Double Fantasy*. These I have found invaluable: the conversations with Andy Peebles for Radio 1, published in book form as *The Lennon Tapes* (BBC); the interviews by David Sheff in *Playboy* and Barbara Graustark in *Newsweek*; and a US radio broadcast issued on CD as *John Lennon Testimony* (Thunderbolt). John also wrote a tremendous memoir, "The Ballad of John and Yoko" compiled in a book of his essays, *Skywriting By Word Of Mouth* (Pan and HarperCollins).

As reference works, two are in a class of their own. Allen J. Wiener's *The Beatles: The Ultimate Recording Guide* (Aurum) covers their solo music in copious detail, while John Robertson's *The Art And Music Of John Lennon* (Omnibus) throws light on even the most neglected corners of Lennon's output. The latter author's chronicle, *Lennon* (Omnibus) is extremely useful, too. A US radio series, *The Lost Lennon Tapes*, made a huge amount of material available for the first time. A warm, convincing portrait of John emerges in May Pang's book *John Lennon: The Lost Weekend* (SPI, written with Henry Edwards); his sometime lover reveals much, without descending into tack or overplaying her role.

For an account of the political background, I'd commend *Come Together: John Lennon In His Time* (Faber & Faber) by the US scholar Jon Wiener. For coverage of John's creativity outside of music, consult *John Lennon: Drawings, Performances, Films* (Thames & Hudson), edited by Wulf Herzogenrath and Dorothee Hansen. There is an excellent chapter on John in Rogan Taylor's study of shamanism and show business, *The Death And Resurrection Show* (Blond). There are two major biographies, of which Ray Coleman's *John Lennon* (Pan) is the fan's choice, being solid and sympathetic; Albert Goldman's attempted demolition, *The Lives Of John Lennon* (Morrow) is horribly readable, if deeply flawed.

Other books that I've found helpful are: *The Beatles: An Illustrated Record* by Roy Carr and Tony Tyler (New English Library); *The Lennon Companion* edited by Elizabeth Thomson and David Gutman (Macmillan); Jan Wenner's *Rolling Stone* interviews, published as *Lennon Remembers* (Penguin); *The Complete Beatles Chronicle* by Mark Lewisohn (Pyramid); *Revolution In The Head* by Ian MacDonald (4th Estate); *Every Little Thing* by William McCoy and Mitchell McGeary (Rock&Roll/Popular Culture Ink); *The Love You Make*, by Peter Brown and Steven Gaines (Pan); *Elvis & Lennon* by Chris Hutchins and Peter Thompson; *John Lennon In My Life* by Pete Shotton and Nicholas Schaffner.

I've drawn also on my interviews with people who knew John Lennon personally. In particular, Paul McCartney has shared lots of memories, and thus deepened my appreciation of his former partner's work. Cynthia Lennon was fascinating to talk to. Other insights came from Bob Gruen, Neil Aspinall, Kieron Murphy, Derek Taylor, George Martin, Pete Best, Tony Barrow and Larry Parnes. I spoke to most of these while working for three of the world's best music magazines — *Q*, *Mojo* and the *NME* — where I had the added benefit of good editors who loved their Lennon: Mark Ellen, Mat Snow and Neil Spencer. Several more friends and colleagues were kind enough to assist me with this book, and I thank Steve Turner, Barry Miles, Ronnie Hughes, Mark Lewisohn, Ian MacDonald, Charles Shaar Murray, Ian Cranna, Jon Savage, Lorraine Dickey at Carlton and, of course, my wife Una.

May you all shine on and on and on.

Paul Du Noyer, 1997

SHINING ON

Lennon's aunt, Mimi Smith, who raised John in suburban respectability.

The world knew him as a man of peace, but John Lennon was born in violence. And he died in violence, too. He came into the world on 9 October 1940, when Liverpool was being bombed to rubble by Hitler's air force. The Oxford Street Maternity Hospital stood on a hill above the city centre; below it were the docks that had made the seaport great, but were now earning it a terrible punishment. Liverpool was Pearl Harbour every night in those war years, and thousands perished in terrace slums or makeshift shelters. But Julia Lennon's war baby survived, and she took it home unharmed. All around them was the din of sirens and explosions.

The Lennons' house was small, in a working class street off Penny Lane; John's father, Freddie, was away at sea. Liverpool was where generations of new Americans took their leave of Europe, and its maritime links with New York stayed strong. Freddie Lennon was like many Liverpudlian men, who knew the bars of Brooklyn better than the palaces of London. "Cunard Yanks" became a source of the US R&B records that made Liverpool a rock'n'roll town. Black American music found a ready market in this port, which had grown rich by selling the slaves of Africa to the masters of the New World. In a park near John's home stood a statue of Christopher Columbus, inscribed: "The discoverer of America was the maker of Liverpool."

John was of the usual local stock, not so much English as Welsh and Irish. The latter, especially, had dominated Liverpool since the mass migrations of the famine years. They gave the Lancashire town a hybrid accent all of its own, which John never lost. The Celtic stereotypes were always applied to Liverpool — violent and sentimental, lovers of music and words, witty and democratic. Far from breaking the mould, Lennon was that stereotype made flesh.

But his upbringing was traditionally British. His respectable Aunt Mimi looked after John from the age of five. With her husband George Smith she raised the boy in a neat, semi-detached house in Menlove Avenue, on Liverpool's outskirts. Post-war

The house on Menlove Avenue, Liverpool, where John spent most of his childhood.

John, with Yoko in their Greenwich Village apartment, indulging in his lifelong passion for drawing.

Britain was still subject to scarcity and rationing ("G is for orange," went John's poem *Alphabet*, "which we love to eat when we can get them"), but his circumstances were comfortable. He had a loving home, and was educated at Quarry Bank, one of the city's better state schools. His background was not as deprived as he sometimes implied.

Yet he could not forget that his natural parents had deserted him. Freddie left Julia, and Julia did not want her infant John. It was not until his teens that John would see his mother regularly, whereupon she was killed in a road accident. The tragedy seems to have compounded John's sense of isolation. As a child, he claims, he used to enter deep states of trance. He liked to paint and draw, and loved the surrealistic, "nonsense" styles of Lewis Carroll, Edward Lear and Spike Milligan. But his quick mind made him a rebel rather than an academic achiever.

To Liverpool suburbanites of Mimi's generation, the city accent meant a lack of breeding, while shaggy hair and scruffy clothes awoke pre-war memories of poverty. John made it his business to embrace all those things.

Rock'n'roll was his salvation, arriving like a cultural H-bomb in mid-Fifties Britain when John was 15. But his musical education began earlier. As Yoko wrote in the sleevenotes to *Menlove Avenue*, a compilation featuring some of John's Fifties favourites, "John's American rock roots, Elvis, Fats Domino and Phil Spector are evident in these tracks. But what I hear in John's voice are the other roots of the boy who grew up in Liverpool, listening to 'Greensleeves', BBC Radio and Tessie O'Shea." As well as the light classics and novelty songs of that pre-television era, John learned many of the folk songs still sung in Liverpool ('Maggie May' among them) and the hymns he was taught in Sunday school. Like his near neighbour Paul McCartney, Lennon's subconscious understanding of melody and harmony, if not of rhythm, was already being formed many years before his road-to-Damascus encounters with Bill Haley's 'Rock around the Clock' and Elvis Presley's 'Heartbreak Hotel'.

By the dawn of the 1960s, when John's old skiffle band the Quarry Men had evolved into Liverpool's top beat group, the Beatles, he'd absorbed rock'n'roll into his bloodstream. The town's cognoscenti were by this time devouring the sounds of Brill Building pop or rare imports of Tamla Motown soul. When Lennon and McCartney made their first, hesitant efforts to write songs instead of copying American originals, their imaginations were a ferment of influences. Country and western was the city's most popular live music, which is why the Beatles' George Harrison became a guitar picker instead of a blueswailer like Surrey boy Eric Clapton. Then there was anything from Broadway shows to football chants, to family memories of long-demolished music halls.

More than all of these, there was Lennon and McCartney's innate creative talent. They inspired each other, at first as friends and then as rivals. Their band, the Beatles, was simultaneously toughened and sensitized by countless shows in Hamburg, the

The early Beatles at the Cavern Club, newly smartened up by their manager Brian Epstein.

Cavern and elsewhere. And in London they met George Martin, who was surely the most intuitive producer they could ever have worked with. Finally on their way, the Beatles were world-conquering and unstoppable.

All this was not enough for Lennon. Millions adored 'Please Please Me', 'She Loves You' and 'I Want To Hold Your Hand', but John soon tired of any formula, however magical. Hearing the songs of Bob Dylan, he was stung into competing as a poet. Turning inwards to his own state of turmoil, he yearned to test his powers of self-expression. He began lacing the Beatles' repertoire with songs of dark portent, such as 'I'm a Loser' and 'You've Got To Hide Your Love Away'. Attempting his most naked statement so far, he wrote a song that he simply called 'Help!' — but the conventions of Top 20 pop music ensured that nobody guessed he meant it.

As the Beatles gradually began to disappear behind moustaches and a sweet-scented, smoky veil, Lennon's lyrics moved towards more complex and original imagery. And yet paradoxically, there was greater self-revelation. 'Norwegian Wood', 'Tomorrow Never Knows', 'Strawberry Fields Forever' – while these songs were often suffused with gnomic mystery, the emotional presence of their creator remained unmistakable. He disdained the everyday, anecdotal songs that had become Paul's hallmark. "I like to write about me," he told *Playboy* magazine in 1980, "because I know me. I don't know anything about secretaries and postmen and meter maids."

His unthinking honesty almost killed him in 1966. A casual comment to a London newspaper — that the Beatles were more popular than Jesus — was shrugged off in Britain but summoned forth a torrent of death threats from America. "It put the fear of God into him," remembers Paul McCartney. "Boy, if there was one point in John's life when he was nervous. Try having the whole Bible Belt against you, it's not so funny." Coming through that, and having resolved the Beatles would not tour any more, John was ready for something else to happen in his life.

What happened was a woman named Yoko Ono. A Japanese artist, she arrived as if from nowhere and revolutionized John Lennon's life. "She came in through the bathroom window," he joked in 1969.

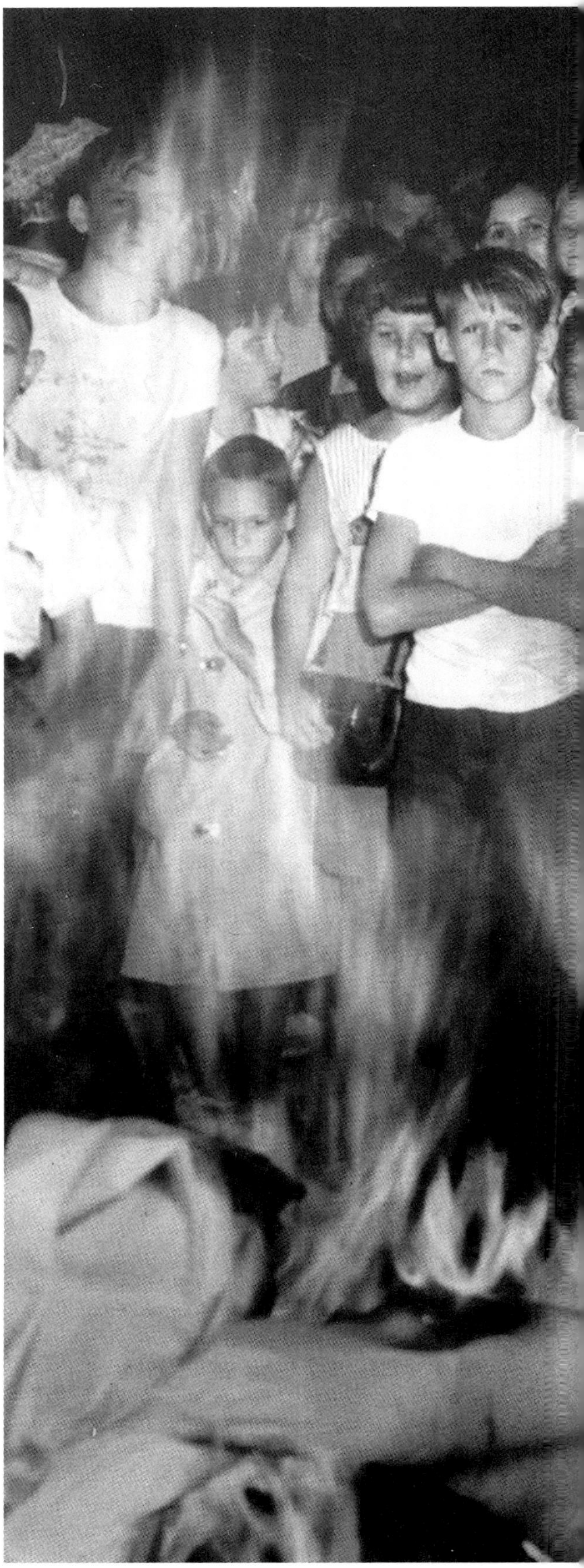

Ceremonial burning of Beatles records at Waycross, Georgia in 1966, following John's "more popular than Jesus Christ" quote.

"She encouraged the freak in me." John divorced his wife Cynthia, the girl he'd dated when they were Liverpool art students, and married the partner he described as "me in drag." Yoko was, in fact, the twice-married daughter of a wealthy Tokyo family, and a seasoned performer in her own right. The art that John understood involved writing words and music, but the key to Yoko's art was its "concept". In her world the idea was more important than the artefact, which could be anything — from a film of a smile to an evening spent onstage in a bag.

In 1968 the couple made an album called *Two Virgins*, more renowned for their nude photo on the cover than for its contents, which were a mosaic of sound effects, conversational snippets and random noise. Around the same time, Lennon used a similar technique for the track 'Revolution 9' on the Beatles' "*White Album*". "John was turned on by it all," says McCartney, who'd introduced John to the work of avant garde composers and shown him some sonic tricks. "Being John, he'd make the record of it. He'd get so excited. 'I've got to do it!' Whereas, being me, I'd experiment but just bring it to our mainstream records.

"John would always want to jump over the cliff. He may have said that to me: 'If you're faced with a cliff, have you ever thought of jumpin'?' I said, 'Fuck off. You jump, and tell me how it is.' That was basically the difference in our personalities… Once he met Yoko he was, 'Ah, we can do it now.' He let out all these bizarre sides to his character. He didn't dare do it when he was living in suburbia with Cynthia, the vibe was wrong. He had to come to my house and sneak vicarious thrills… John picked up on all of this because he was now with Yoko and Yoko would say, 'This is very good art, we must do this.' She gave him the freedom to do it. In fact she wanted more. 'Do it double, be more daring, take all your clothes off.' She always pushed him. Which he liked — nobody had ever pushed him before."

Yoko and John were married in March 1969, just a week after Paul and Linda McCartney. The timing symbolized an accomplished fact. The two men had ended the central partnership of their youth, as they commenced the key relationships of their maturity. Neither woman had an easy ride from press and public thereafter, but Yoko's was the harder. At one extreme there was anti-Japanese abuse; but there was also scepticism about her talent, and disapproval of her influence on John. But in spite of what many felt she did not break up the Beatles — they were disintegrating of their own accord.

To his credit, John defended her at every turn. In the face of ridicule and hostility, they even made more records together. In May 1969 there was *Unfinished Music No. 2: Life with the Lions*, featuring distorted guitar and unearthly vocals; its second side carried a faltering heartbeat, in honour of the child they lost in a miscarriage. Their *Wedding Album* was released in November — another baffling collage of sounds. They never lost an opportunity to proclaim their love for one another, although, as John confessed that same year, "Even with two people who are as lucky as us and have somebody that can be close on all levels, there's still great depths of misery to be found. That's the human condition and there isn't any answer for that."

It was a common assumption in Britain that Yoko had "stolen" John for his money and fame. But the years that followed seemed to bear out an observation by the Beatles' last manager Allen Klein, that John needed Yoko more than she needed him. All we can say is that every couple is a private universe, and as outsiders we can only speculate. His ready wit and common touch were always a curious contrast to her stiff, esoteric image. But he chose her, could not operate for very long without her, and produced as many great songs after he met her as he did before.

The experimental records he made with Yoko were revealing — as everything John produced was revealing — but we can date his career as a solo songwriter to 1969, when 'Give Peace a Chance' was credited to the Plastic Ono Band. The group existed only in theory, named after a Yoko project involving plastic models of musicians, wired up to perform on stage. In the end the Lennons only ever made the models in miniature, but the Plastic Ono Band did exist as an ad hoc pool of players, sometimes even including George and Ringo, with John and Yoko at its nucleus. His first non-Beatle records overlapped with the Beatles' final releases, but by 1970 he was out there on his own.

"We all shine on!" Lennon performs 'Instant Karma!' on British TV in early 1970.

"Bagism", one of the more unorthodox tactics in John and Yoko's 1969 peace campaign.

There was a scattering of public appearances, whether bed-ins, bag-ins or orthodox concerts. The most important was at a rock'n'roll revival show in Canada, which spawned the album *Live Peace In Toronto 1969*, with John and Yoko being joined by Eric Clapton, the Beatles' old Hamburg comrade Klaus Voorman and drummer Alan White. Strung out on heroin, John rehearsed his instant band on the plane going over, and they played a ramshackle set of Fifties cover versions, some of Yoko's elongated improvisations and the first performance of 'Cold Turkey'. Nothing preoccupied him more, though, than his campaign for world peace, for which he and his wife were willing to play "the world's clowns" and be "the court jesters of the youth movement."

It was John's *Imagine* album, in 1971, that finally won him credibility as a rock star outside of the Beatles, but it was the last record he made in England. Never a great lover of London, he found his ultimate home in New York City, where Yoko recalls him gazing nostalgically at the docks and piers and the Atlantic liners, and declaring it was "like a Liverpool that has got its act together." A few more years of bustle and upheaval preceded his virtual retirement in 1975, a turning point marked by the birth of his son Sean. He wrote to his friend Derek Taylor, "I meself have decided to be or not to be for a coupla years… I ain't in a hurry to sign with anyone or do anything. Am enjoying my pregnancy… thinking time…what's it all about time too."

A lurid picture of John's last years was painted by the author Albert Goldman in *The Lives Of John Lennon*. But Goldman was, perhaps, unduly taken with his previous, masterly description of Elvis Presley's decline. His book sacrificed warmth and sympathetic understanding in an effort to show John's seventh-floor Dakota apartment as a decadent Graceland-in-the-sky. Our final sightings of John Lennon were not of a ravaged man. He was thinner and older — but then, he had never looked especially young — while his manner was gentle and contented, as if he'd found the equilibrium which had eluded him all his life.

Unlike most Sixties stars, John showed in his final songs that his powers were not failing him in middle age. He was gunned down in 1980, and it's still a bitter thought that his development was arrested by such a freakish act of hatred. In an age when fame is thought to be all-important, no matter how it is earned, his assassin Mark Chapman must count as some kind of success story.

Ever since that moment, Lennon's impact has been endlessly debated. The impulse of some fans to see him as a martyr, and to shroud him in piety, is surely misguided. It has incited others to react against this saintly aura and to rubbish his gifts to posterity. Fortunately, we still have his music, which was always a reliable guide to John's true nature, in all its human fallibility and occasional moral heroism. Lennon was maddeningly inconsistent. He turned ideological cartwheels in a casual way that made his allies despair. His personality underwent transformations worthy of a B-movie werewolf. He could be the most abject prisoner of self-pity, or else a husband and father uplifted by familial love. And there is Lennon music to illuminate every step of that journey.

Sometimes, John did not so much hold ideas as wear them, like Kings Road clothes. The finery that delighted him in summer would bore him by the fall. Perhaps that was his job — not to be consistent, necessarily, but to sift suggestively through the thoughts and dreams that swirled about the world in his time. He was so receptive that he often seemed gullible. But he was fearless, too. He lived his life on thin ice, and usually over boiling water. He was a radar who picked up anything in the air and then, being the holy fool he was, rushed to put it into practice. He enacted his times dramatically.

Believer and cynic, alternately muddle-headed and clear-sighted, brash and vulgar, vulnerable and compassionate — Lennon cannot be simplified or denied. Yoko Ono commented, aptly, "They say that a blind man has an honest face," because he has never learned to use his expressions to tell a lie. In this way she liked to explain the helpless candour shining through John Lennon's songs. Whatever he felt or experienced could not remain concealed, because there was always music to be made and John would unburden his soul to the world. It's a burden, however, that can be a joy to carry.

12 JOHN LENNON/ PLASTIC ONO BAND

SINGLES

'Give Peace A Chance'
'Cold Turkey'
'Instant Karma!'

ALBUM

JOHN LENNON/
PLASTIC ONO BAND
'Mother'
'Hold On'
'I Found Out'
'Working Class Hero'
'Isolation'
'Remember'
'Love'
'Well Well Well'
'Look At Me'
'God'
'My Mummy's Dead'

John and Yoko introduce their 'conceptual' group, the Plastic Ono Band, to a bewildered audience at London's Lyceum Theatre, 15 December 1969.

On a British TV programme at the end of 1969, John Lennon found himself nominated as Man of the Decade, though he had to share this distinction with John F. Kennedy and the North Vietnamese leader Ho Chi Minh. As the new decade opened the Beatles were virtually finished as a recording entity and their split would soon be made public, culminating in a messy tangle of lawsuits. Yet John's personal fame and notoriety were at an all-time high.

A series of well-publicised events served to keep him in the news alongside his inseparable partner Yoko Ono. Chief among these was the second of his "bed-in" protests, held in a hotel suite in Montreal, at which he performed a new song, 'Give Peace a Chance', and began to emerge as a recording artist in his own right. This single became the most memorable mass-anthem of its era, but in artistic terms it was only the prelude to an exceptional series of releases that established him as a solo star.

Behind the hullabaloo of his media career, and despite the profound attachment he had formed to his new wife, John's inner existence was as fraught as it had ever been. His second single, 'Cold Turkey', spoke openly of his heroin addiction. Its lyrics lay bare his private torment, with a frankness he could seldom express while writing underneath the Beatles' umbrella.

If the third Lennon single 'Instant Karma' opened the 1970s on a magnificent note of optimism, then his new album, *John Lennon/Plastic Ono Band*, was undeniably bleak. Its cycle of ravaged laments dwelt obsessively in a realm of psychic pain. For many fans it stands as John's masterpiece, although it is probably an album more admired than enjoyed. Tracks explore Lennon's ambivalent attitude to stardom, the mental scars of his childhood, the traumas of the Beatles' break-up and his lifelong struggles to find spiritual meaning and a sense of himself.

After he issued 'Cold Turkey', whose imploring words and grimly discordant sounds amount to a cry of anguish, he was sent *The Primal Scream*, a book by the American psychiatrist Dr Arthur Janov. It's no wonder that Janov's work struck Lennon to the core of his being. It was *The Primal Scream*'s contention that an adult carries the scars of his earliest upbringing. Only by uncovering and confronting those scars can we progress to an existence free from neurosis. These were ideas that John had been groping blindly towards for many years.

He undertook a lengthy course under Janov's instruction, but was obliged to leave the US when his visa expired. To that extent his treatment remained incomplete, but the experience inspired him to write an album's worth of self-revelatory material, trying to drive out his demons. The 'Instant Karma' single had inaugurated his partnership with the great producer Phil Spector, with whom he now made an album of unrelenting starkness, utterly unlike the lavish extravaganzas for which Spector was renowned.

At EMI's London studios in Abbey Road, the cradle of nearly all the Beatles' music, John and Yoko began work on two parallel solo albums on 26 September 1970. Yoko's was a relatively un-structured affair, but John's new songs were some of the most sharply focused he would ever create. Using a stripped-down team consisting of Ringo Starr on drums and the Beatles' old Hamburg friend Klaus Voorman on bass, with some piano embellishments from Billy Preston and Spector himself, John completed his record in a little over four weeks of intensive effort. Released just before Christmas 1970, the record's back sleeve carried a grainy snapshot of John as a small boy — as if to acknowledge that old proverb, The child is father to the man.

The five-year-old Lennon at Dovedale Primary School, a year after his mother had left him.

GIVE PEACE A CHANCE

Locked out of the United States — he was refused a visa on account of his 1968 drug conviction — John chose Montreal, Canada, as a base to bring his peace campaign to North America. Denied his first choice of the Plaza in New York City, on 26 May 1969 he and Yoko installed themselves in a suite of the Queen Elizabeth Hotel for a seven-day "bed-in", attended by the world's media, show business celebrities and sundry hangers on. This bed-in was their second such event, following the one staged at the Amsterdam Hilton after their wedding two months earlier. Its origins lie in Yoko's days as a performance artist, and the notion that spectacular public action can be an art form in itself. John, too, was shrewdly aware of how the "bed-in" concept might titillate the press and TV crews with its implicit (though ultimately unfulfilled) promise of sexual exhibitionism.

"Just give peace a chance," he kept telling

"Just give peace a chance," John kept telling reporters at his 1969 "Bed-In" events at Amsterdam and Montreal. The words grew into the anti-war anthem he had dreamed of writing.

reporters, and began to work the refrain into a song.

By 1 June John felt he had a powerful peace anthem on his hands, and ordered up a tape machine. Still in bed with Yoko, with a placard behind them proclaiming "Hair Peace", he invited all his varied guests (including the LSD guru Timothy Leary, comedian Tommy Smothers on guitar, singer Petula Clark, a local rabbi and several members of the Montreal Radha Krishna Temple) to sing along to his new composition. 'Give Peace A Chance' was a chugging, repetitive mantra, interspersed with John's impromptu rapping, a babbled litany of random name-checks (ranging from the novelist Norman Mailer to the English comedian Tommy Cooper) and impatient dismissals of "this-ism, that-ism". The rapping was a decade ahead of its time. But it was not of primary importance, for this was another of John's "headline" songs (in the tradition of 'All You Need Is Love' and 'Power To The People') whose deliberately simplistic chorus mattered far more.

Released under the banner of the Plastic Ono Band on 7 July, 'Give Peace A Chance' was John's first single outside of the Beatles. Yet it still carried the composer credit "Lennon & McCartney" in

accordance with the partners' longstanding pact. John confessed later that he was not ready to sever links with Paul, and also felt a degree of guilt because he was the first to issue a major record outside of the group. Explaining its muffled double drumbeat, he said, "My rhythm sense has always been a bit wild, and half way through I got on the onbeat instead of the backbeat, and it was hard because of all the non-musicians playing with us. So I had to put a lot of tape echo to keep a steady beat right through the record."

John Lennon's disenchantment with the Beatles deepened in 1969, with relations made worse by his addiction to heroin.

Years later, he revealed, "In my secret heart I wanted to write something that would take over 'We Shall Overcome'." And, in 'Give Peace A Chance' he achieved just that. By October of 1969 the song was a universal chant at anti-Vietnam War demonstrations. On 15 November nearly half a million people sang it outside the Nixon White House in Washington. Such a coup would store up trouble for John in subsequent dealings with the US administration. But when he watched the protestors singing, on his TV back in Britain, he considered it "one of the biggest moments of my life". At the year's end he told interviewer Barry Miles, "There's a mass of propaganda gone out from those two bed-ins... Every garden party in this summer in Britain, every small village everywhere, the winning couple was the kids doing John and Yoko in bed with the posters around... Instead of everybody singing 'Yeah Yeah Yeah' they're just singing 'Peace' instead. And I believe in the power of the mantra."

'Give Peace A Chance' was to enter the world's consciousness more completely than any other song John wrote. Eleven years later, as mourners gathered outside the Dakota Building on the night of his murder, this was the song that they instinctively chose to express their grief and commemorate his life.

COLD TURKEY

Drugs are by no means unknown in the lives of many rock musicians, yet the subject is seldom addressed directly in songs. Typically, John was one of the first to break that taboo, and did so in a song that is still extraordinarily vivid in its raw depiction of suffering. After the LSD which fuelled the psychedelic dreamtime of the *Sgt Pepper* album in 1967, Lennon's experiments with drugs led him on to heroin. He would wrestle with its potentially fatal attraction for years to come. In August 1969, driven by his desire to conceive a healthy child, John made another determined effort to quit the drug, and wrote 'Cold Turkey' as a document of the process. He does not glamourize his self-abasement.

Tittenhurst, the elegant Georgian manor occupied by John and Yoko from 1969 until their move to New York in 1971. Two years later they sold the house and park to Ringo Starr.

In the latter half of 1968, when John had finally abandoned his wife Cynthia and the family home at Kenwood, he and Yoko took up temporary residence at Ringo's old flat in Montagu Square. According to an interview she gave to former personal assistant Peter Brown, Yoko admitted to having dabbled with heroin while John was away in India with the Maharishi earlier that year. It seems almost inevitable that he would have become curious to try it for himself.

There was a certain innocence surrounding all forms of drug taking in the 1960s, when few people were aware of its dangers, or thought themselves immune in any case. And John was drawn by heroin's reputation as an "artistic" indulgence. His attachment grew throughout 1969 when the couple moved into their grand white mansion, Tittenhurst Park in Ascot, and there is little doubt that it contributed to his further estrangement from the Beatles.

Like other inexperienced users, John was dismayed to find how difficult it was to stop taking heroin. Reluctant to use a hospital, for fear of the attendant publicity, he tried at first to break his addiction by abrupt abstinence — the method called "cold turkey". The physical effects resemble a feverish illness — two of the most common symptoms are clammy skin and goosebumps, hence the name. They are graphically described in John's verses.

The song was at first considered for recording by the Beatles, who were then completing the *Abbey Road* album. Not surprisingly it was rejected, its content so harrowing and so personal that it could only be a Lennon solo project. John premiered the number at the Toronto Rock'N'Roll Show on 13 September, backed by the hurriedly formed band that included Eric Clapton on guitar. Throughout, John cribbed from a lyric sheet held up by Yoko at his side. It was the only new song of John's that they attempted that night, and the crowd's reaction was muted, prompting him to snap at them, "Come on, wake up!".

Clapton was duly called to EMI's studio in Abbey Road a few weeks later to help with the single. Playing to a pattern that John had devised, and recalling the monstrous, violently distorted style of the previous year's 'Revolution', Eric contributes the searing guitar riff which is among this record's most compelling and brutal characteristics. It's ironic to note that Clapton would, within a year, be in the grip of a prolonged heroin habit himself.

But the most startling element of all is John's vocal performance, probably his most extreme since 'Twist and Shout' six years before. He claimed the howling style was derived from Yoko, and it certainly pre-dates his discovery of the "primal scream" therapy explored on his subsequent solo album, whose themes are also anticipated in his whimpering wish to be a baby again.

Unhappily John's self-prescribed treatment was not a success. On his birthday, 9 October, the pregnant Yoko was admitted to hospital and suffered a miscarriage three days later. He relapsed into heroin use thereafter.

'Cold Turkey' was released in the middle of October, credited to the Plastic Ono Band. Its subject matter and sheer harshness guaranteed that media exposure would be limited, and the record was not a big hit. Hence the jokey pay-off in John's letter to the Queen when he returned his MBE (Member of the British Empire, a royal honour bestowed upon all four Beatles in 1965) on 25 November: "Your Majesty, I am returning this MBE in protest against Britain's involvement in this Nigeria-Biafra thing [a civil war then raging in West Africa], against our support of America in Vietnam and against 'Cold Turkey' slipping down the charts. With love, John Lennon of Bag."

In Britain at least, this gesture generated even more controversy than 'Cold Turkey' itself. Still, the single played its part in dismantling the Beatles' public image. Given the trouble John was already in with the authorities over drugs, he might have been wise to avoid the subject in song. But as a writer — if not always as a man — honesty was John Lennon's greatest addiction of all.

Newly-decorated Beatles at Buckingham Palace, 26 October 1965. John did not take his MBE seriously, and returned it to the Queen in mock protest at 'Cold Turkey's slide down the pop charts.

INSTANT KARMA!

Famously impatient, John once longed "to write a song on Monday, cut it Tuesday, have it pressed Wednesday and in the shops by Friday." He nearly realised that ambition with 'Instant Karma!' A pure example of John's fast, reactive method of songwriting, it may also stand as the most uplifting rock song of his solo career.

Yoko and John spent the New Year of 1970 in Denmark, visiting her daughter Kyoko and the child's father Tony Cox. While there the couple took the unexpected step of cutting off their long hair, and now faced the world sporting unisex crops. Seemingly they had decided to usher in the new decade by abandoning a look whose symbolic power had dwindled. (The locks were later auctioned for one of the couple's pet causes.) Meanwhile in John's absence, on 4 January, the other three Beatles convened at Abbey Road to complete Paul's song 'Let It Be'. It proved to be the group's final recording session.

▲ **The Lennons greet the Seventies. Photographed in Denmark by Yoko's ex-husband Tony Cox, the couple presented their freshly-cropped heads to a startled world.**

Back in London by late January, John wrote 'Instant Karma!' in a single morning, building around a simple riff with a passing resemblance to 'Three Blind Mice'. The title phrase was something he had picked up in conversation with Tony Cox's new wife, Melinde Kendall, in Denmark. Hippies of the 1960s had absorbed the Hindu doctrine of "karma" in line with their general receptivity to oriental ideas and music — encouraged largely by the Beatles themselves and George in particular. In time, Western usage tended to trivialise karma, until it meant roughly the same as "just deserts", either good or bad. But in its original context the word referred to a man's deeds across a cycle of lifetimes, and to their consequences for his ultimate spiritual fate.

"Instant" karma, then, is a contradiction in terms. But how typical of John to want the concept compressed into something more immediate. The slow-turning wheel of existence was just not his speed. What excited him was that karma could refer not only to past actions affecting us now, but also to our present actions shaping the future, and faster than we think. Fascinated by the language of advertising, he loved the idea of selling Instant Karma in the same way as instant coffee. Parallel with this message — take responsibility for the fate of the world, and do it now — went the song's central theme, that stardom is a quality we all possess, famous or not. The only real stars are up in the heavens, but the potential for spiritual brilliance comes with being human. It is not the gift of an élite. "We all shine on."

These are majestic sentiments and, though its tune is unambitious, the finished song does ample justice to them. For this we can thank Phil Spector. 'Instant Karma!' was John's first collaboration with rock'n'roll's most legendary producer, and it is a sonic triumph. Contacting Spector was the final coup in a productive day that had seen John write his song and round up a studio band comprising George Harrison, Klaus Voorman and Alan White. It happened that Spector was visiting London to discuss involvement in the Beatle tapes that would become their *Let It Be* album. The record that Lennon and Spector cut at Abbey Road this evening marked the start of an historic two-year partnership. With its commanding, echoed vocals and the almighty wallop of White's drumbeats, 'Instant Karma!' was the definitive sound of post-Beatles Lennon; he would deliberately evoke it ten years later, in '(Just Like) Starting Over'.

Harnessing the additional lung power of revellers from a nearby nightclub, 'Instant Karma!'s sound was built up in layers, in the classic Spector tradition, until it reached monumental stature. His "Wall of Sound" technique, evolved in the making of landmark Sixties hits such as 'Be My Baby', 'Da Doo Ron Ron' and 'River Deep Mountain High', required the same instrumental parts to be played many times, with the results allowed to reverberate around the studio. A typical Spector record gave the impression of cavernous space, as if created in some vast cathedral of pop. John was content to tell Spector he wanted "a 1950s feel," and left the rest in his producer's hands. Like Lennon, Spector preferred to think of records in terms of total sound, not as collections of component details. Heretically, he even disdained the advent of stereo, coining his own slogan "Back to Mono".

'Instant Karma!' was released in Britain on 6 February, barely two weeks after it was written, and on 20 February in the States. British fans received another treat on 12 February when John appeared on the nation's TV weekly institution *Top Of The Pops*, the first Beatle to do so since 1966. While he hammered the piano, with an armband on his denim jacket saying "People for Peace", Yoko was perched behind him, blindfolded, holding up cards with simple inscriptions such as Peace, Love, Smile and Hope. Not unusually in the career of John Lennon, much of the population decided he had gone mad, but the song's almighty, thudding drumbeat and its soaring, inspirational chorus were sufficient to give him a Top 5 hit.

John never became blasé about chart positions, and was gratified by the success. But 'Instant Karma!', like 'Give Peace A Chance', had a wider purpose. He wanted to change people's minds. "The government can do it with propaganda," he reasoned. "Coca-Cola can do it with propaganda, the businessmen do it with propaganda. Why can't we? We are the hip generation." The essence of 'Instant Karma!' he once insisted, was to breathe belief into people. "All we're trying to say to the world is, You're gonna be great."

John's absentee father, Freddie Lennon, made a bid for pop stardom in 1966, with an autobiographical single called 'That's My Life'. Still embittered by his desertion, John offered no help.

MOTHER

A horror movie on TV provided John with the idea for the funereal bell whose ominous toll — even gloomier when slowed down by Phil Spector — is the curtain-raiser to *John Lennon/Plastic Ono Band* and its opening track 'Mother'. Looking for pure gut-feeling, Lennon interrupted the session to play a disc of Jerry Lee Lewis's manic stomper 'Whole Lotta Shakin' Goin' On'. John traced much of his unhappiness back to a sense of rejection by his parents. And now, to free himself of that baleful legacy, he must in turn say "goodbye" to them. Yet, by the song's wracked finale, he is screaming at Mummy not to go, and begging Daddy to return.

The real life events which left John so bereft are well-documented. His mother, Julia, felt ill-equipped to raise him. Almost as soon as he was born she disowned his father, Freddie Lennon, who was in any case absent from home for long periods, serving as a merchant seaman. On his return Freddie made a bid to take the infant John away with him. Amid all of the turmoil at home, the child spent several spells in the care of relatives. At the age of four he was finally placed with Julia's elder sister Mimi and her husband George Smith. He saw little of his real mother until his teenage years, when Julia's own rebellious nature and playful spirit drew her son closer. In adolescence he certainly found her more of a soul mate than the deeply suburban, eminently respectable Mimi. He began spending more of his time with Julia, while she encouraged his musical ambitions by allowing him his first cheap guitar.

But when John was 16 their gradual reconciliation was cruelly and abruptly terminated. Following a visit to Mimi's house, Julia was knocked down and killed by a car driven by an off-duty policeman. As John reflected later, "I lost her twice."

Freddie, meanwhile, disappeared from the boy's life entirely. He got back in touch after John won fame as a Beatle, by which time Freddie was hard up and working in a series of dead-end jobs. At one

With his wife Cynthia, fellow Beatles and other celebrities, Lennon spent the early months of 1968 at the Maharishi's retreat in India. But his later songs reeked of disillusionment with gurus.

point he even tried to launch himself as a recording star: his single 'That's My Life" was the self-celebrating tale of a Liverpool seafarer. Their relationship was uneasy and marked, on John's part at least, by hostile recrimination, though he did make financial provision for his father. Freddie fell seriously ill in the Seventies, after John had moved to New York, but father and son apparently had a series of affectionate phone conversations in the days before the old man's death on 1 April 1976.

Given John's unsettled background, it is often suggested that he sought a father-figure in later life, with his managers Brian Epstein and Allen Klein, or even the Maharishi being proposed as substitutes. In a 1972 interview with *Record Mirror* John appeared to endorse that theory: "Three years ago I would have been looking for a guru or looking for the answer in Karl Marx, but not any more. I was looking for a father figure but I do not want that any more thanks to Dr Janov. He gave me a kind of structure and I do not need him any more. He helped me to accept myself."

It's striking, too, that he always called Yoko "Mother", albeit in a semi-mocking tone. "I've got the security of Yoko," he told Barry Miles in 1969. "And it's like having a mother. I was never relaxed before, I was always in a state of uptightness, and therefore the cynical Lennon image came out." 'Mother' was one of the few solo songs that John ever played in public. At Madison Square Garden in 1972, he was anxious to widen the lyric's scope: "People think it's just about my parents. But it's about 99 per cent of the parents."

HOLD ON

The naked terror of 'Mother' is genuinely disturbing, and shows the depth of John's commitment to Janov's teaching at that point. But it's balanced by declarations of tenderness such as 'Hold On'. A shimmering, Japanese-influenced riff introduces this short exercise in gentle reassurance. When John had surveyed the outer world's chaos, in his 1968 song 'Revolution', the best advice he could offer was, "It's gonna be all right". He repeats that message here, sustained in his faith by the nourishment of love. Speaking of Yoko in 1969 he said, "Now I can remember, even in the worst depths of misery, that we're both going through it together." With a little belief, he tells his audience, we can come through our confusion and achieve a feeling of unity, with one another and within our own personalities. It's arguable that John was singing more out of hope than experience. Nevertheless, many who knew him testify that he became a more approachable character after meeting her. And 'Hold On' chimes agreeably with another Lennon aphorism from that year: "We're all frozen jellies. It just needs somebody to turn off the fridge."

I FOUND OUT

After the tranquil yearning of 'Hold On', Lennon turned his unsentimental gaze on the forces that he believed were dangerous distractions from our quest for self-understanding. Lined up for curt condemnation are radical hippies, drugs, sex and religion. The scornful put-downs are framed with an arrangement of effective viciousness, and John was especially proud of his truculent guitar playing on this track. But Ringo's drumming is the most exciting feature of all, like the pounding of an agitated heart as it echoes the singer's bitter glee.

Successive verses list the various snares that John has identified, now he has "found out" that liberation is something he will only attain though his own resources. First in his firing line are the "freaks on the phone," imploring John's support for their chosen causes. There is no doubt that John became a figurehead for radically-minded people, whether of the hippie "counterculture" or more orthodox political activists. His phenomenal celebrity, his presumed wealth and anti-establishment sympathies made him a natural target for anyone who might benefit from his attention.

Like all show business figures, he was accustomed to begging letters, usually from strangers pleading poverty, illness or exceptional ill-fortune. The ghastliness of the Beatles' world tours had been compounded when sick children and abject invalids were presented to the group for their imaginary healing powers. The band's Apple label, initially conceived as a tax advantage, naïvely announced a philanthropic agenda and fast became a magnet for no-hopers and hip scroungers of every description. In fact John did make regular gestures of support — in February of that year, for instance, he paid the fines of 100 protesters arrested in demonstrations against a UK visit by the South African rugby team. Clearly, however, he had his breaking point and constant appeals of the "brother brother brother" sort had worn him down. In 'I Found Out' it is not the money he begrudges, but the claims on his time and mental energy.

He also launches a broadside against religion. For someone who had never really embraced the Church he would devote a lot of effort to repudiating it. In the 1968 song 'Sexy Sadie' he had already registered his disillusionment with the Maharishi, but gurus and "pie in the sky" come in for further abuse here. His position may sound absolute, but this was a debate that John would never quite resolve in his own mind. Like so much of *John Lennon/Plastic Ono Band*, his outburst represents a temporary clearing of the mental decks more than a definitive statement.

The early loss of their mothers was a bond that had drawn John closer to Paul McCartney in the Beatles. In Lennon's case, though, there was the added element of rejection, fuelling his desire for fame. The reference here to his mother and father, whose rejection "made him a star", is explained by a comment he made in 1971: "The only reason I went for that goal is that I wanted to say, 'Now, mummy-daddy, will you love me?'."

WORKING CLASS HERO

The title of 'Working Class Hero' is sarcastic rather than narcissistic. Lennon writes as someone whose dreams have all come true, only for him to realise that those dreams were just illusions. The song talks of a numbness instilled by social conditioning. Encouraged by Janov's teachings, John examined his schooldays for evidence that his talents were suppressed by teachers and concluded that only conformity is rewarded. We are all levelled down, he argues: the clever ones are hated and the stupid are despised. He goes on to borrow some ideas then current among left-wing intellectuals, chiefly that freedom and the classless society are myths designed to obscure our basic lack of power over our lives, while the media, commercialized sexuality and drugs, legal or otherwise, likewise conspire to blunt our appetite for social change.

John and Yoko married in Gibraltar on 21 March 1969. Their romance became the central theme of Lennon's solo work.

The minimal delivery of this song, with its threadbare acoustic strumming, induced many comparisons to Bob Dylan. While John had openly adopted Dylan as an important role-model during the Beatle years, he became irritated by the frequency of these comparisons, responding that the solo acoustic style was a feature of folk music long before 'Blowing In The Wind'.

As a self-portrait of Lennon in his most cynical mood, 'Working Class Hero' is unsurpassed. He performs it with a morbid fatigue that reeks of his own disillusionment. He has made a success of his life, he implies, but only on the narrow terms defined for us — mainly money, fame and self-indulgence. We are easily controlled, his thesis runs, because we allow our imagination to be curtailed. But these themes are not particularly obvious, and the title 'Working Class Hero' would go on being applied to John without any shade of satire, or else be taken as a sign of his egotism. He told *Rolling Stone*'s Jann Wenner that he hoped the song would become an anthem "for the workers", with the same appeal as 'Give Peace A Chance'. But its meaning proved much too elusive.

ISOLATION

Between the grand announcements and the dramatic peaks of *John Lennon/Plastic Ono Band* come the more modest numbers such as 'Isolation', a momentary pause for John to plead quietly of his own vulnerability. However celebrated he may be, or reviled, he is an individual like any other, as tiny in relation to the universe and just as imprisoned within his own existence. In Lennon's case his isolation was something he sought as well as regretted. He spoke of his wish to belong, but recognised a contrary impulse to stand apart. As a Beatle he came closer than anyone to global popularity, yet at times he seemed hell-bent on throwing it away.

When he developed a campaigning platform in 1969, he saw there was a certain freedom in playing the clown. "I'm not a politician," he told *Oz* magazine, "so I don't rely on public opinion as to how I run my life — I refuse to. I mean, I don't even consider it. For a politician to go into a white bag in the Albert Hall he'd have to consider the effects it would have on his constituents, but I'm not a politician and I don't owe my constituents anything other than that I create something, whatever it is, and they accept or reject it on its own merits."

While it's not among his better songs, 'Isolation' transcends the well-worn "lonely at the top" trap because it is sufficiently general to describe a feeling which is apt to settle on most people at one time or another.

REMEMBER

The jogging piano rhythm of 'Remember' is reminiscent of Paul McCartney's contribution to John's song 'A Day In The Life', conferring some urgency on what is otherwise a song of no great purpose. If the point of primal therapy was to scrape away the archaeological layers of his memory, 'Remember' settles on a series of disconnected flashbacks, coupled with a formulaic call to harbour no regrets. Much as Lennon felt compelled to escape the psychic burden of bygone times, he was actually nostalgic to an unusual degree. 'Strawberry Fields Forever', named for a place where he played as a child, is the most famous instance. In 'She Said, She Said' he mourns his boyhood, when "everything was right"; in 'Help!' he draws a similar contrast between the untroubled past and his anxious present, while 'In My Life' leafs wistfully through Lennon's back pages. It's interesting that he numbered each of these backward-looking songs as being among his best works.

The final line, a seemingly climactic call to "remember the Fifth of November" was a mere afterthought. It quotes the rhyme traditionally sung by British children on that date, Guy Fawkes Night, when fireworks and bonfires celebrate the foiling of a 17th century plot to blow up the government. John probably relished the allusion, hence the huge explosion dubbed on to the song's ending, but its appearance here owes more to chronic nostalgia than revolutionary fervour.

LOVE

Phil Spector plays the delicate piano line of this tender, uncomplicated ballad, whose sweetness anticipates the next album *Imagine*. In 1980 John recalled this song with some affection, no doubt because it conjured up one of the more harmonious periods in his marriage to Yoko. He was often inclined to dismiss his angrier songs as being rooted in guilt or self-hatred, or as instances of some transient discontent, whereas the romantic numbers maintained their appeal for him. In fact he cited 'Love' with 'Imagine' itself as two of the compositions he considered as good as anything he'd done with the Beatles. Whether we agree with that estimation or not, 'Love' is a welcome addition to this generally tortured album, and a useful reminder that Lennon's real life was never a one-dimensional affair.

WELL WELL WELL

A clenched, grunge-like guitar figure combines with some of Ringo's toughest drumming in this depiction of vignettes from John and Yoko's day to day existence. Amorous interludes are described, with due account given of the tensions they felt when they addressed the world outside their own private universe, building into a bout of savage, rasping hollers. At one point John finds his wife so beautiful he "could eat her" – an improvement on his first draft, "she looked so beautiful I could wee."

LOOK AT ME

The piano was John's chief songwriting instrument for his early solo albums, but 'Look at Me' is based around acoustic guitar picking. In this it betrays its origins in 1968, when it was among the batch of songs he wrote with the Beatles' "*White Album*" in mind, others of the type including 'Julia', 'Dear Prudence' and 'Cry Baby Cry'. Therefore it dates from a time of crisis in John's love life, when his passion for Yoko was leading him to leave his wife Cynthia. The warmth of the song is accordingly tempered by John's confessions of deep uncertainty. Only when he had resolved this doubt and committed himself to Yoko could he begin to rebuild his sense of identity. The essence, then, of 'Look at Me', is the story of a man who comes to believe that his only true existence is in his lover's eyes.

GOD

Both Mother' and 'Working Class Hero' are among the most outstanding tracks on *John Lennon/Plastic Ono Band*, but 'God' can justly be called the album's centrepiece. The rippling piano introduction interweaves with stately chords that seem to be announcing that a Grand Statement is the way. And so it is, for in 'God' we get John Lennon's most explicit exposition of his outlook in summer 1970, just two months on from the official break up of the Beatles which had been confirmed by Paul's walk-out on 10 April.

The song begins with a fairly consistent tenet of John's religious thinking, namely that God is an abstraction who really resides within human beings themselves. He then repeats the assertion for good measure. Having disposed of the biggest, he then proceeds to list each lesser concept in which he is no longer prepared to invest his faith. Magic, the occult and mysticism are dismissed. Jesus, Buddha, the Kennedys, monarchy, Elvis Presley, Bob Dylan (alias "Zimmerman", his real name) are likewise dispatched while the track lurches forward, gathering in force as it unrolls. But the most impassioned disavowal of all — and in many ways the most shocking — is reserved for last. He does not, he declares, believe in Beatles.

Like 'A Day in the Life' before it, 'God' is a uniquely structured song. The litany ends abruptly, to be succeeded by a dramatic pause and, then, a quiet affirmation of his one remaining certainty. He believes in himself, and in himself with Yoko. The final and most poignant passage delivers his final summing up: "The dream is over." Calmly and even coldly, he buries the Beatle myth and counsels all of us, Beatle fans and former Beatles alike, to leave him in peace.

In all, it amounts to a majestic abdication. He has formally renounced his position as leader of the band who once embodied the dreams of a decade and as the icon of a generation. John always resented the impression that Paul had broken up the Beatles, and insisted it had been his decision. McCartney's press announcement caught him on the hop. If John could not be the first to break the news, he now wanted the distinction, at least, of issuing the most resounding public obituary. From now on, he would say, we were on our own. He later encapsulated the message of the Beatles' era as "Learn to swim" — acquire the spiritual self-sufficiency that life demands, without recourse to gurus, politicians or pop stars.

John with his first wife, Cynthia, before he met Yoko Ono in 1966. By the middle of 1968 his marriage to Cynthia was finished.

Bob Dylan is among the icons toppled in Lennon's song 'God'. But his deep influence on John was evident in 'Working Class Hero'.

The Beatles never did re-form during John's lifetime. But he did rekindle some of the mystical interests so roundly rubbished in 'God', including tarot, yoga and mantra, as well as developing some sporadic enthusiasm for social activism. In its entirety, then, 'God' is best understood as what Yoko called "a declaration of independence", part of John's continuing search. In true primal scream fashion, he was cleansing his brain of anything and everything that stood between him and the core of his being. 'God' illuminates the process whereby John hoped to rediscover himself as a man, not as a Beatle, in order that he might begin his life all over again.

MY MUMMY'S DEAD

American psychiatrist Dr Arthur Janov, whose book *The Primal Scream* inspired the soul-baring intensity of John's first solo album.

The album's brief closing track is just about the simplest composition that John ever committed to record. It's also the scariest, and all the more chilling for the blankness of John's delivery, like that of a man whose grief has drained him. It is therefore an appropriate end to the primal scream experience, John having purged himself to the point of emptiness, the better to start afresh. Naturally, 'My Mummy's Dead' serves to "bookend" the record, referring back to the first song 'Mother'. Julia's death is here recalled as an event so awful that John could never display his hurt.

He often ascribed his youthful anger to the repressed emotions he felt at his mother's killing. Eerily the song resembles a ghostly transmission from the distant past — played as if on a toy guitar, with rudimentary chords, crudely recorded as if on a primitive tape machine in John's boyhood bedroom. The child-like lyric, he later said, was plain and short because he wanted to write his own form of "haiku", meaning a Japanese three-line poem. The true haiku is highly artificial, written to contain a precise number of syllables, but it may convey a profound observation. Although Lennon could never work to such a disciplined remit, he had a bluesman's ability to express his intimate feelings with the most basic of musical tools.

13 IMAGINE

SINGLES

'Power To The People'

ALBUM

IMAGINE
'Crippled Inside'
'Jealous Guy'
'It's So Hard'
'I Don't Want To
Be A Soldier'
'Gimme Some Truth'
'Oh My Love'
'How Do You Sleep?'
'How?'
'Oh Yoko!'

The Lennons with Yoko's daughter Kyoko. Their fight for custody of the child would lead them from England to New York, never to return.

John completed 1970 with a trip to New York, promoting his "difficult" solo album to a doubting marketplace. He began 1971 with a first visit to Yoko's family in Japan. He had played to tougher audiences, but not many.

Meanwhile, in the High Court in London, lawyers picked over the mortal remains of the Beatles, as the ex-members issued ill-tempered statements that were a far cry from the palmy days of 'All You Need Is Love', or even of 'Give Peace A Chance'. Under the growing influence of the British underground, John composed a marching song entitled 'Power To The People'. To raise a fighting fund for the movement's house journal, *Oz*, he also wrote a single, 'God Save Us'/'Do The Oz', recorded by Bill Elliott & The Elastic Oz Band.

By June, John and Yoko were back in New York, continuing their quest for custody of Yoko's daughter Kyoko, who was still in the care of Tony Cox. While there, they met Frank Zappa and impulsively joined him on stage that very night, at the Fillmore East. Some of the gig — perhaps a little too much — would appear on a live disc with John's later album, *Some Time In New York City*. On the same visit, John fell under the spell of America's star radicals Jerry Rubin and Abbie Hoffman. He would renew this acquaintance later in the year, when he returned to America to live.

The remainder of that summer was spent at the Lennons' English country home, Tittenhurst Park, whose many gracious amenities now included a home recording studio. Here they invited Phil Spector, and musicians including George Harrison, Klaus Voorman and Alan White, to make the basic tracks for John's new album, *Imagine*. A young Irish photographer, Kieron Murphy, watched the cast assembling in John's kitchen: "They'd been recording all night and sleeping through the day. When I got there it was 5 o'clock in the afternoon and he was having breakfast. I remember being amazed at seeing him tuck into bacon and eggs: I thought, People who are this famous eat more rarefied foods...."

Of the legendary Spector's arrival, Murphy says, "It was almost as if he'd come up out of the floor in a puff of smoke. He had a very heavy presence. He just seemed to arrive without coming into the room. And the interesting thing was that John looked almost as in awe of Spector as I was of John. He leapt up to give him his chair, fussed around him and got him tea or coffee. Everybody else is being a bunch of boisterous lads, swapping football stories and whatever, but Spector just sat there...

"Then Spector says to him, very quietly, 'John, I think we should make a start.' Whereupon John leapt to his feet and literally took the cups of tea out of people's hands, frogmarching them into the studio: 'Phil wants us now!' I was amazed to see that John Lennon had to obey anybody."

When *Imagine* finally appeared, in September of 1971, the title track enchanted the world with its idealistic plea for universal altruism. Other songs continued to examine his inner doubts, and his adoration of Yoko in the face of widespread ridicule. One track, 'How Do You Sleep?' simply tore into Paul McCartney. Whatever its contents, though, *Imagine* pleased the public because it was melodic, lushly arranged and kind on the ears — qualities its predecessor, *John Lennon/Plastic Ono Band*, had never been accused of.

John, of course, was less certain he had done the right thing. He often criticised the album for its softness. In 1974 he assessed its merits this way: "I prefer the 'Mother'/'Working Class Hero' than *Imagine* myself... I suppose anything you do is either better or worse than something or other, I mean, that's how we seem to categorise things... 'This fish tastes as good as the fish we had in St Tropez, but not as nice as the one Arthur caught off Long Island, on the other hand, do you remember that fish and chip shop in Blackpool?'."

POWER TO THE PEOPLE

During the Montreal bed-in which spawned 'Give Peace A Chance', John mocked the US government for considering him a political militant: "I think they might think I'm gonna hot up the revolution. But I wanna cool it down." Yet the next 18 months would see him drift away from smiley-badge pacifism, and closer to the hardline "agitprop" (or agitation/propaganda) of the Maoist left wing. Once again he immortalised his passions of the moment in an overnight anthem. The slogan was an old one, but John's adoption of "Power To The People" would propel the phrase into everyday use. Within a few years, it would be claimed not just by socialists, but by virtually anyone from right-wing conservatives to advertising copy writers. In short, it would become meaningless.

In January 1971 John had returned from his trip to Japan with Yoko. Once more installed in the palatial setting of Tittenhurst Park, he gave an interview to the intellectual duo Tariq Ali and Robin Blackburn, representing the underground leftist magazine *Red Mole*. Ali, in particular, had been big in the 1968 student protests which provoked John's song 'Revolution'. Back then, John could not decide how far he supported revolutionary ideas, especially if they

A pro-democracy supporter defies government tanks during the Peking protests of June 1989. Yoko saw a parallel between these events and John's anthem 'Power to the People'.

meant people got hurt. One version of 'Revolution' appeared on the Beatles' "*White Album*", and John fudged his stance by singing "count me out, in". But another version, released as the B-side to 'Hey Jude', has him telling the agitators they can count him "out".

By the time of his Ali/Blackburn audience, two-and-a-half years later, John is finally prepared to enlist in the movement. In the interim, conservatives had regained political power both in Britain and the US (Edward Heath's Tories and Richard Nixon's Republicans, respectively). Youthful opposition to government acquired a more strident tone. Lennon tells his interviewers he has always been a working class socialist at heart. He regrets that 'Revolution' did not make his allegiance clear. Yoko pleads for non-violent revolution, but John is doubtful: "You can't take power without a struggle." He talks with pleasure of hearing Beatle songs such as 'All Together Now' and 'Yellow Submarine', and his own 'Give Peace A Chance', being taken up by football crowds, or in pubs or on demonstrations. "That is why," he goes on, "I would like to compose songs for the revolution now."

The *Red Mole* men left Tittenhurst Park, doubtless satisfied by the superstar's submission. As good as his word, John went straight to work on a song inspired by their conversation. 'Power To The People' is both battlecry and threat. Exploited workers are urged to take to the streets. Their capitalist exploiters are warned, "We got to put you down." Another verse enjoins his comrades and brothers not to overlook the rights of their womenfolk. It was Yoko who introduced John to feminism; in 1971 it was not an automatic item on the average street fighting man's agenda.

By the next day, 22 January, he was in the studio with his bopping manifesto, but again it was Phil Spector's efforts which made all the difference. To the swirling sax of ace sessioneer Bobby Keyes, Spector added a full-blown gospel choir for righteous conviction. Next he multi-tracked the sound of the musicians' tramping feet. But then he whipped the whole number up into something that was far lighter on its feet, much more supple and funky, than the basic composition implied. It was the first ever call to mass proletarian action that you could dance to – a feat that Lenin never achieved, but Lennon did.

'Power To The People' came out in America on 22 March. The original Yoko B-side, 'Open Your Box', was replaced with another of her songs, the more romantically-titled 'Touch Me'. As it climbed the charts, London's High Court witnessed the ongoing collapse of the Beatles into squabbling factions.

Lennon was not proud of 'Power To The People'. He came to regard it as "a guilt song" done to appease the radicals who assailed his rich man's conscience. Actually, he dismissed it as "shit". But the song's central sentiment can assume fresh relevance. In a 1992 video compilation, Yoko put the track to footage of the Chinese pro-democracy demonstrations in Tiananmen Square.

GRAPEFRUIT
YOKO ONO

IMAGINE

Paul McCartney's 'Let It Be' and Paul Simon's 'Bridge Over Troubled Water' had, almost simultaneously, struck a pseudo-religious note in the 1970 hit parade. John was openly contemptuous of 'Let It Be', but he was to write the third of these definitive rock hymns himself. 'Imagine' is probably the most widely-revered of all John's songs, including those by the Beatles. Here, at least, he bettered Paul, whose solo work could never surpass a song like 'Yesterday' in popular affections. The restful opening notes of 'Imagine' still strike a deep chord in people of all beliefs. Strangely, not even its explicitly secular message has stopped the song becoming a favourite at modern-minded religious events.

But the currents that run through 'Imagine's lyrics are muddy, as was Lennon's attitude to the Christian faith he was raised in. "I'm a most religious fellow," he told *Playboy* in 1980. "I only now understand some of the things that Christ was saying in those parables." As a child he attended Sunday School and sang in the choir. Christian hymns would have been his first formal engagement with music, just as the Christian God was the first philosophical concept he had to wrestle with. Therefore the church-like tenor of 'Imagine' was quite natural for him, especially as he composed it on the piano rather than the guitar. And the subjects it covers — from the existence of God downwards — were themes that nagged at him for years.

As the lyrics unfold we are asked to imagine a universe *sans* heaven or hell, and a world where people live for the day instead of the afterlife. Religion, like nationhood, is cited as a cause of conflict. Can we imagine ourselves without them, or material possessions, and living in global harmony? He'd ended his previous album by declaring that "the dream is over". He begins this one by announcing a new dream, and inviting us to share it. There was something nearly clairvoyant too in John's critique of national boundaries. The US immigration service would become the bane of his life, and the fight for US citizenship his longest-running battle.

'Imagine' has its origins in Yoko Ono's book of poems, *Grapefruit*, published in 1964. In it, Yoko begins each poem with a similar invocation. Thus, *Tunafish Sandwich Piece* starts, "Imagine one thousand suns in the sky at the same time...". *Rubber Piece* begins, "Imagine your body spreading rapidly all over the world like a thin tissue...", and *Cloud Piece* is quoted on the album sleeve itself: "Imagine the clouds dripping. Dig a hole in your garden to put them in." John would later say that he should have given Yoko a co-writer credit for the song. But, he told *Playboy*, "I wasn't man enough... I was still full of wanting my own space after being in a room with the guys all the time, having to share everything."

The second source of inspiration was a prayer book given to John by the US comedian Dick Gregory. Advocating "positive prayer", the book advised that to receive anything from God, we must first imagine it for ourselves. This idea impressed John greatly. The day before he died he was still expounding "projection of our goals". If we wish for a positive future we should exert our mental energy and visualise one. In 1980 he observed how this idea, once considered wacko, was now being adopted by everyone from business organisations to sports stars. If we conceive of the future as something violent, like *Star Wars*, then we run the risk of creating precisely that.

Sitting in the spacious white music room of his agreeable English manor, imagining "no possessions", Lennon was soon accused of hypocrisy. But his Utopian dream, with its wistful existentialism, tapped a vast reservoir of feeling in the post-War world. The song has become a standard. John's own opinion was typically perverse. He stood by *John Lennon/Plastic Ono Band*, believing it more "real" than anything else he'd done. But the softer tones of 'Imagine' represented compromise, or even sell-out. "Imagine was a sincere statement," he told *NME*'s Roy Carr in 1972. "It was 'Working Class Hero' with chocolate on. I was trying to think of it in terms of children." When Paul McCartney was so incautious as to praise 'Imagine', Lennon quickly fired back: "So you think 'Imagine' ain't political? It's 'Working Class Hero' with sugar on for conservatives like yourself."

Signing copies of Yoko's book, *Grapefruit*, at the London store Selfridges in 1971. John used these poems as the basis of his new song 'Imagine'.

CRIPPLED INSIDE

After the claustrophobic meditations of *John Lennon/Plastic Ono Band*, the *Imagine* LP was more inclined to poke its head above the parapet and satirise the world outside. It was certainly much brighter, musically. While 'Crippled Inside' is really rather dark in content, and quite as self-lacerating as its predecessors, John presents it as the jolliest of knees-ups. Its lyric is no more than a warning that we cannot use externals — whether they be rhetoric, religion or nice clothes — to disguise our fundamental problems. But he deploys a battery of musical jokes to make the observation sparkle. Ragtime piano, reminiscent of American vaudeville or an English pub singalong, skips and twinkles over George's slide guitar, itself a nod to the country-funk style brought to rock's mainstream by the Band. As a song, 'Crippled Inside' goes nowhere but it gets there with considerable charm.

JEALOUS GUY

'Jealous Guy' began its life a few years earlier as 'Child of Nature', but was not used by the Beatles. Perhaps it clashed with Paul's title, 'Mother Nature's Son', which was unveiled at the same session and duly appeared on the group's "*White Album*". 'Jealous Guy' in its finished form was a keynote song of John's maturing outlook, expressing his rejection of the macho values he had grown up with. In later interviews he was frank about his violent tendencies, though he believed he had brought that side of his nature under control. In his youth he fought often. Indeed some of his earliest press coverage arose from an incident at Paul's 21st birthday party in Liverpool when John attacked and hospitalized his old friend, the Cavern DJ Bob Wooler, for accusing John of a gay encounter with the Beatles' manager Brian Epstein, whom he'd just accompanied on a brief holiday in Spain.

Worse yet, John confessed that he had been violent towards women. He told *Playboy*, "I was a hitter. I couldn't express myself and I hit. That is why I am always on about peace… I will have to be a lot older before I can face in public how I treated women as a youngster." Jealousy was the usual reason for his outbursts, a tendency revealed in his Beatle song 'Run For Your Life', in which he describes himself as a "wicked guy" with "a jealous mind", before copping a line from his hero Elvis Presley's 'Baby Let's Play House', where he warns his girl he'd rather see her dead than with another man. And John admitted the truth of a line he'd given to Paul's breezy *Sgt Pepper* song 'Getting Better' — he really was cruel to his woman, to the point of beating her up.

'Jealous Guy' begins with a suggestion that John's latest transgression is a lapse into his bad old ways, born of his insecurity. His relationship with Yoko was always stormier than the couple preferred to indicate — it's said that he made her list her former lovers, and resented her knowing Japanese because it removed so much of her consciousness from him. But in 'Jealous Guy', one of his most persuasive melodies and Spector's airiest arrangement, the eloquence of John's repentance carries all before it.

John's first wife Cynthia saw plenty of John's volatility, especially during their early courtship in Liverpool. But she doubts that he ever changed entirely, nor needed to: "He was really never a macho working class man, John. I think his talents were above and beyond that. He was like a chrysalis. He had to be macho to cope with some of the types he came across in Liverpool. He tended to try to look like the tough guys so that the tough guys wouldn't pick on him. So what John became was what John really was, underneath it all."

In the melancholy winter months after John's death, Roxy Music's sensitive reading of 'Jealous Guy' became a worldwide hit, one of the finest musical tributes ever paid to its composer.

Elvis Presley in 1956, when John's admiration was at its peak. By the time of 'Jealous Guy', however, Lennon was disavowing his macho rocker heritage.

IT'S SO HARD

If the fragile 'Jealous Guy' depicted a wild man looking for the gentler side of his nature, then the following track, 'It's So Hard', asserts that Lennon has not forgotten how to rock. A grinding blues boogie, of the sort that thick-ankled rock bands were excessively fond of back then, it has a crunch like truckwheels over gravel, and some epic Fifties saxophone. It's not a statement of anything much, confining itself to John's stoic observations on the everyday demands of life, love and work. Lennon was never one to make existence easier for himself — quite the contrary — but he reserved the right to complain loud and long whenever it got too much.

'It's So Hard', however, is more of a boastful swagger than a self-pitying whinge. And the stomping grunginess of its basic track is magically uplifted by Spector's added strings, hovering in the light, Hollywood-Oriental style that he and John became so fond of. Spector had suffered a few lean years since his hey-day in the Sixties, and seemed to relish the new album's spaciousness.

The photographer Kieron Murphy remembers being invited back to Tittenhurst Park to hear the finished *Imagine* album. He found John anxious about the public's response, after the cool reception given to his previous album. But 'It's So Hard', like the next track 'I Don't Want To Be A Soldier', cheered him up hugely, thanks to their inclusion of the legendary sax-player King Curtis, overdubbed by Spector in New York. "He was really proud," reports Murphy. "It was, 'We managed to get King Curtis!'. He didn't seem to get that people would kill their own mothers to play on one of his albums."

John, though, had every reason to be humble. As one of England's first connoisseurs of rock'n'roll, he would have revered "King" Curtis Ousley, whose tenor sax defined The Coasters' 'Yakety Yak' and dozens of Atlantic R&B classics. Just prior to the *Imagine* sessions, Curtis had played for Aretha Franklin and formed his own band featuring the Beatles' sideman Billy Preston. But only a month later, on 15 August 1971, Curtis was stabbed to death by a vagrant, on the front steps of his New York home. We may understand John's awe when we read the producer Jerry Wexler's tribute to the saxophone giant: "Six foot one, powerful, cool and radiant… Curtis was noble, ballsy and streetwise like nobody I ever knew."

'It's So Hard', then, seems a pretty good epitaph.

The legendary sax player King Curtis. He made a key contribution to *Imagine* but was brutally murdered a few weeks later.

I DON'T WANT TO BE A SOLDIER

It's hard to envisage a more unlikely candidate for military discipline than John Lennon, so the sincerity of 'I Don't Want To Be A Soldier' may be taken as read. The song had more resonance, perhaps, for young American fans, to whom Vietnam and the draft were a real issue. But, during John's childhood, Britain too had its relic of wartime conscription, in "National Service" for young men. To John's immense relief the scheme was

'I Don't Want To Be A Soldier': Lennon wore khaki only for the 1966 satirical movie *How I Won The War.*

The luckless Badfinger: Tom Evans (left) and Joey Molland (right) played on *Imagine*, but Evans and Pete Ham (second right) were later driven to suicide.

abolished just before he became eligible. "I remember the news coming through," he told Barry Miles,"that it was all those born before 1940, and I was thanking God for that as I'd always had this plan about Southern Ireland (*which was outside of UK jurisdiction*). I wasn't quite sure what I was going to do when I got to Southern Ireland, but I had no intention of fighting." In his interview with *Red Mole* he claimed he had been brought up "to despise the army as something that takes everybody away and leaves them dead somewhere."

The closest John ever to got to wearing uniform was the cover of *Sgt Pepper*, or in his role as Private Gripweed in Richard Lester's movie *How I Won The War*, though he also took to affecting guerilla fatigues during his radical phase of the early Seventies. But Lennon never forgot, or forgave, Presley's spell in the military. "Elvis died when he went into the Army" was his terse response to the King's passing in 1977.

The song's structure was loosely built around the nursery rhyme, "Tinker, tailor, soldier, sailor. Rich man, poor man, beggarman, thief." Lawyer and church man are likewise cited as careers he was keen to avoid. Echoing to the heavens, Phil Spector's production pulls out all the stops, including King Curtis's saxophone squalls and a fusillade of rock guitar. Some of the latter was contributed by Joey Molland and Tom Evans from the Beatles' Apple protégés Badfinger. This band's fate proved as unhappy as King Curtis's — their founder Pete Ham, and Tom Evans himself, later hanged themselves after a succession of business setbacks. Ironically, the gifted pair were responsible for writing 'Without You', a massive hit for John's great friend Harry Nilsson.

▲ **Richard Nixon meets Elvis at the White House on 21 December 1970. Presley advised the President that the Beatles were "a real force for anti-American spirit." He also offered his services as a narcotics agent, and presented Nixon with a handgun.**

GIMME SOME TRUTH

By now an avid observer of the political scene, John took grave exception to "Tricky Dicky" Nixon whose escalation of the Vietnam War made him Public Enemy Number One among liberals and radicals. John's exasperated demand for honesty prefigures the Watergate scandal, which only served to confirm his worst suspicions about the President.

The bare bones of 'Gimme Some Truth', however, could be discerned as early as January, 1969, when the song was attempted at the Beatles' Twickenham sessions, most of which wound up on the *Let It Be* album. It's therefore likely that John's initial rant against deceit was born of the Beatles' internal disputes. As such, it was practically a parallel track to Paul's wistful *Abbey Road* complaint, 'You Never Give Me Your Money'.

It's unknown whether Nixon ever heard John's blistering tirade, but the singer's general disposition was well-known to the White House, as can be seen from numerous official documents. Even if they'd missed the message, they were advised of Lennon's "subversive" proclivities by the all-American patriot Elvis Presley, who urged the administration to act against the outspoken Beatle. It's an inglorious episode in the King's career — but then, as John's biographer Chris Hutchins noted wryly, "If Elvis had succeeded in having him banned from the United States, he would still be alive today."

OH MY LOVE

Jointly credited to Yoko, 'Oh My Love' is another number with its origins in the batch that John prepared for the Beatles' 1968 "*White Album*". A brief, gentle song of awakening tenderness, it sits demurely in between two of *Imagine*'s most enthusiastic bouts of personal abuse. One man who observed John and Yoko's blossoming romance at close hand was Paul McCartney: "In the Sixties," he reflects, "you thought, If I'm gonna go with this person for the rest of my life, like John and Yoko or me and Linda, I really ought to look them in the eye all the time. John and Yoko really did spend a lot of time (*he mimes comically intense eye contact*) and it got fairly mad, looking at each other going, It's gonna be all right, it's gonna be all right, it's gonna be all right. After a couple of hours of that you get fairly worn out."

John took pride in having picked Paul McCartney and Yoko Ono as the two creative partners of his career. The London premiere of *Yellow Submarine*, in 1968, was a rare display of public solidarity.

▲ **Lennon and McCartney in more harmonious times, on a TV shoot in 1963. John's symphony of spite, 'How Do You Sleep?' marked the lowest point of their relationship.**

HOW DO YOU SLEEP?

For all the sweetness of its "chocolate-coated" arrangements, *Imagine* has its share of vitriol, and the bitterest song of all was John's blatant assault on Paul McCartney, 'How Do You Sleep?'. Amid the legal gunsmoke enveloping the defunct Beatles, relations between the old friends had sunk to an all-time low. In May, a month before the *Imagine* sessions started, Paul released his second solo album, *Ram* — replete, or so John thought, with underhand attacks on him and Yoko.

True, the cover art includes a photo of a pair of beetles, arguably "screwing" one another. And the music opens with Paul apparently crooning, "Piss off, yeah." But to most people's ears the *Ram* lyrics were innocuous, vague and downright throwaway. Still, John detected malice in lines such as "We believe that we can't be wrong", "Too many people preaching fantasies" and the allusion in '3 Legs' to a friend who has let him down.

John and Yoko at Tittenhurst in June 1971, as they began recording *Imagine.*

Whatever McCartney's intentions, there was to be no such obscurity in John's counter-attack. The original *Imagine* LP was even issued with a postcard showing John grappling with a pig, in mockery of the Ram cover where Paul had displayed his rustic aspirations by posing with a sheep. So far, so childish. But 'How Do You Sleep?' really took the gloves off. Drenched in a deceptively gentle string setting, the song begins with a parody of *Sgt. Pepper*'s opening and proceeds to lambast McCartney as a baby-faced lightweight, a man who "lives with straights" who fawn on him, and a writer whose only achievement was 'Yesterday'. "Since you're gone," sneers John, in a slighting reference to Paul's admittedly feeble new single, "you're just Another Day."

The latter line was offered to John by Allen Klein, the New Yorker brought in to oversee the Beatles' business affairs, in the teeth of opposition from Paul. On this occasion, however, Klein was not goading John to greater excesses of spite, but rather saving him from potential libel — his original couplet, according to biographer Albert Goldman, alleged Paul had probably lifted the tune of 'Yesterday' anyway. There is something almost endearing in the way that the *Imagine* album can range from the highest aspirations of global consciousness-raising to the tiny-minded bickering of the school playground. In accusing McCartney of "Muzak", John knew that he could depend on hip opinion to back him up. But in Lennon's populist heart, it still rankled that Paul's melodies still possessed the common touch.

Elsewhere John jeers that the "freaks" were right to say that Paul was dead. This refers to the hoax perpetrated by an American radio station in 1969, when myriad "clues" were read into the Beatles' lyrics and album sleeves, supposedly revealing that the current McCartney was an impostor, the real Beatle having died in a 1966 car crash. This ingeniously elaborated rumour enjoyed a wide circulation. Why, for example, did Paul's *Sgt Pepper* costume include a badge saying "O.P.D."? Surely it stood for "Officially Pronounced Dead"? And doesn't John conclude 'Strawberry Fields Forever' with the words, "I buried Paul"? (Alas for conspiracy theorists, that O.P.D. badge came from the Ottowa Police Department, while John's actual words were "cranberry sauce".)

Photographer Kieron Murphy, who was present at the session, recalls there being no discussion of the song's lyric, but notes that Yoko sat at John's feet, writing down the words. "He was literally making the album up as he went along, and he was teaching it, playing it for them. I thought at first it was a slag off of the fans because the first line is 'So Sergeant Pepper took you by surprise.' But it began to click when he sang, the only good thing you did was 'Yesterday' and so on."

The track aroused instant controversy. *Rolling Stone* condemned it as "horrifying and indefensible… a song so spiteful and self-indulgent that it sanctified the victim and demeaned the accuser." McCartney refrained from any musical retaliation. In fact his next album, *Wild Life*, seemed to carry a conciliatory song to John, in 'Dear Friend'. But he did comment, "I think it's silly. So what if I live with straights? I like straights. I have straight babies. It doesn't affect *him*. He says the only thing I did was 'Yesterday'. He knows that's wrong. He knows and I know that's not true."

Paul could draw some comfort from subsequent events. Within a few years the other three Beatles were themselves at daggers drawn with Allen Klein, and John would duly snipe at him in song. By the time John made his last album, of course, he was hymning the praises of domesticity and investing in farm animals — just two of the McCartney traits he'd so smugly satirised. By 1980 John's old grudges were, in any case, subsiding. He said that 'How Do You Sleep?' had not been a personal attack. He compared the song to Dylan's vindictive 'Like A Rolling Stone' — just a pouring out of all his anger, directed at himself as much as anyone else. Well, maybe. More likely is that 'How Do You Sleep?' was one more instance of John's tendency to shoot first and ask questions later.

HOW?

Emerging, as it did, in between the revolutionary broadsides of 'Power to the People' and *Some Time In New York City*, the *Imagine* album represents a pause in John's career as counter-culture spokesman. Whenever he did speak out, he had the gift of sounding completely convinced. Yet he was prone to interludes of doubt, and 'How?' describes one such hiatus. Apart from its ornate orchestration, this track would sit logically inside the previous album, for its themes are old friends — lack of direction, fear of the future, emotional incapacity.

OH YOKO!

Jangling piano, wheezy harmonica and lolloping drums combine to make this the album's breeziest moment. Its chorus is a whoop of joy. Arriving at the record's end, 'Oh Yoko!' has the effect of dedicating the whole of *Imagine* to her. So it's strange, therefore, that John's earliest rehearsals of this song were slow and subdued — almost the work of a nervous man calling for reassurance. Lines like "In the middle of the night, I call your name" take on a mood of bright exuberance, but were written in a darker hour, by a man who was no stranger to fear.

Unsurprisingly, in its final state 'Oh Yoko!' was a very popular track and John was advised to release it as a single. Commercially it would make a fine antidote to agitprop shanties and explorations of inner angst. But John resisted the idea. As he told *Playboy*, "I was shy and embarrassed, maybe because it didn't represent my image of myself of the tough, hard-biting rock'n'roller with the acid tongue." And so a hit was missed. But worse, much worse, was to follow.

The Lennons at home, 1971. *Imagine* songs such as 'Oh Yoko!' marked a rare, though short-lived, period of domestic tranquillity.

14 SOME TIME IN NEW YORK CITY

SINGLE

'Happy Xmas
(War Is Over)'

ALBUM

SOME TIME IN NEW YORK CITY

'Woman Is The Nigger
Of The World'

'Attica State'

'New York City'

'Sunday Bloody Sunday'

'The Luck Of The Irish'

'John Sinclair'

'Angela'

The Lennons spent their radical-chic phase in this cheap apartment in Greenwich Village, before moving uptown to the Dakota.

▲ **Abbie Hoffman, addressing a 1970 anti-war protest. He and Jerry Rubin encouraged John's radical tendencies on his arrival in America.**

Nobody realised, when John left England for New York City on 3 September 1971, that he would never see his homeland again. The US government kept trying to revoke his visa and deny him full resident status, but he stalled them long enough to get his own way. An unfortunate side-effect of the fight was that he was scared to leave the States in case he could not get back in. But the ultimate irony of Lennon's life was that he loved New York and was determined to settle there, because he believed this city would leave him in peace.

There were other attractions, too. "A big Liverpool" was John's fond tag for New York City. The parallels were real enough when you got away from Manhattan's midtown glamour — a couple of tough old seaports, self-obsessed and self-mythologising, where Irish-featured stevedores barked in accents that practically overlapped ("Youse guys over dere, shift dis."). He never stopped comparing the two cities, and both felt like home — only London, which represented the Beatle years in between, was unreal.

At first, September's trip was just another shuttle in John and Yoko's nomadic routine. Still pursuing legal custody of Kyoko, Yoko's daughter by her previous husband Tony Cox, they set up camp in a luxury suite on the 17th floor of the elegant St Regis Hotel, on 55th Street. A few weeks later they rented a tiny apartment downtown, in the altogether funkier district of Greenwich Village.

The immigration squabble conspired to keep John in New York, even if the Kyoko case faded from his agenda. But the situation suited him. For years in England he'd lived nowhere but the stockbroker belt,

Some Time in New York City **came with bonus live tracks from the "Peace for Christmas" show in London, when the Plastic Ono Band had included George Harrison, Eric Clapton and Keith Moon.**

in isolated mansions. Suddenly he found himself at the heart of things. Moreover, he felt accepted. "New York remains the centre of the universe for me," he said. He fell in quickly with the radical gang, like Chicago Seven defendants Jerry Rubin and Abbie Hoffman. They were Yippies (that is, of the Youth International Party) and their playful tendencies were far more congenial to John than the heavy Marxist austerity of European thinkers like Tariq Ali and Robin Blackburn.

John held court in Greenwich Village. White Panthers dropped by and Black Panthers sent their regards. His peacenik Christmas single, 'Happy Xmas (War Is Over)' was already out of step with John's new mood, for these years had seen the two-fingered peace sign fold inside the clenched fist salute. He'd appear on street demonstrations and pose for photos in the sort of hard hat worn by rioting Japanese students. Instead of posting acorns for peace, he'd bawl through megaphones about the IRA.

Like a lot of New Yorkers, he rather played up his remote Irish heritage. Likewise he'd romanticize his slim links with the Liverpool proletariat.

As we've learned in later years, John's enemies by now included Richard Nixon, J. Edgar Hoover and Elvis Presley. But the irony is that John had the makings of a classic American patriot, because he was a fervently grateful immigrant. Where Europeans might revere their native soil for its history, most Americans honour theirs for its opportunities. "I profoundly regret that I was not born an American," he said. He could feel the awesome power of New York to absorb any kind of human being or human activity. As for Britain, its antipathy to Yoko made him even more scornful of its provincialism.

From such a new sense of liberation came one rather poor album. *Some Time In New York City* tackled a range of contemporary issues (feminism, Northern Ireland, black activism) with dogged sincerity rather than artistic inspiration. Nor was it entirely John's record — Yoko contributed several tracks of her own. Although her songs ('Sisters, O Sisters', 'Born In A Prison' and 'We're All Water') were more orthodox affairs than previously, their appeal is still limited. John could take his pick of New York's musical expertise; instead he picked a radical bar band, Elephant's Memory, whose roughhouse energy enchanted him. More ominously, Phil Spector's role was reduced to overseer of the final mixes.

There was a bonus disc, *Live Jam*, from two sources. First was a December 1969 gig by the "Plastic Ono Supergroup" at London's Lyceum. Billed as a "Peace for Christmas" event, the night saw John and Yoko joined by a sprawling cast including George Harrison, Eric Clapton and Keith Moon. They performed an efficient 'Cold Turkey', with John declaiming in his best postcard-from-Hell fashion. Next came a challenging 15 minutes' worth of 'Don't Worry Kyoko', which we may listen to for the same reason people climb Mount Everest – because it's there. Amid the chaos a horn section labours stoically. The remaining tracks are from John's surprise appearance at Frank Zappa's Fillmore East show, in June 1971. Easily the best of these is 'Well (Baby Please Don't Go)', a game take on the old Olympics B-side, introduced by John as "a song I used to sing when I was at the Cavern in Liverpool". Yoko wails in a strange but interesting counterpoint. Three more free-form cuts — 'Jamrag' (an old Liverpool vulgarity), 'Scumbag' and 'Au' — are gruelling and aimless.

Some Time In New York City appeared in America in June 1972; British release came three months after. Its artwork was a pastiche of the *New York Times*, indicating John's crush on "headline" songs, written at journalistic speed — mistakes and all — in reaction to the day's events. Its reviews were nearly all poor and John was back on the defensive. "I tried to make my songs uncomplicated so that people could understand them," he told Roy Carr. "Now they're openly attacking me for writing simplistic lyrics. 'I Want To Hold Your Hand', that was simplistic. If I want more praise I can write more things like 'I Am The Walrus' and songs full of surrealism... There was one criticism that said, 'Please write us some images, not the way you're saying it now.' Well, all I've got to say to people like that is, Get drunk or whatever it is you do. Lay on a bed. Make your own damn images."

But the world was still softly humming *Imagine*, and had no time for *Some Time In New York City*, which sold badly and, more damning, soon became prominent in the second-hand racks. John's "front page songs" had the immediacy that he craved, but not the durability. They became, to quote the Rolling Stones, "yesterday's papers". By 1975 John had admitted as much, remarking that his real job was poetry, not journalism. In his self-conscious effort to reach the masses, he had succeeded in reaching fewer people than ever before.

▲ **One of the billboard messages placed in major cities around the world as part of the Lennons' 1969 peace campaign.**

HAPPY XMAS (WAR IS OVER)

The Beatles used to make a special Christmas record for their Fan Club each year, normally a cheerful package of jokes and jingles. But John hankered after something more substantial. He'd already penned a series of bespoke anthems: 'All You Need Is Love', 'Give Peace A Chance' and 'Power To The People'. That left one ambition unfulfilled. "I always wanted to write a Christmas record," he confessed. "Something that would last forever." In 'Happy Xmas (War Is Over)' he succeeded easily. Back in his homeland, at least, it became a Yuletide family favourite, and the last great populist singalong he was responsible for.

He already had the perfect accomplice in Phil Spector, for this small, furtive figure was a past master at hanging tinsel around rock'n'roll. In 1963 the producer had assembled his roster of hit acts, including the Ronettes, the Crystals and more, conducting them through souped-up versions of 'White Christmas', 'Frosty The Snowman' and so forth. All performed in Spector's hyperbolic, teen-symphonic style, these cornball songs coalesced into one of pop's most wonderful albums, *A Christmas Gift for You*, otherwise known as *Phil Spector's Christmas Album*.

'Happy Xmas (War Is Over)' was the first of John's New York recordings, made in October 1971, his first full month as an American resident. He began by asking Spector to replicate the backing of 'Try Some, Buy Some', a recent single by Phil's wife Ronnie Spector (of the Ronettes), written by George Harrison. Accounts differ, but Lennon remembered the session as a "beautiful" experience; Spector requisitioned children from the Harlem Baptist Choir to enhance the song's community feel.

The chorus was not new. Back in December 1969, at the height of their peace campaign, John and Yoko paid for billboard posters in 11 world cities, declaring "War Is Over! If You Want It. Happy Christmas from John & Yoko." Among the sites selected were Times Square, Piccadilly Circus, Sunset Strip and the Champs-Elysées. The message was translated into the relevant local language, and followed up by a second poster, saying simply "We Want It." These starkly arresting public statements were a type of performance art in themselves.

With the disaster in Indo-China dragging on, John and Yoko felt their message had not lost its relevance. Most important was the "If you want it" component, which echoes the 'Imagine' theme of a future depending on our collective ability to visualise it. John reiterated his belief in the "projection of goals" in his 1980 *Playboy* interview. Peace, he said, was our responsibility and could not be assigned to some outside agency: "We're just as responsible as the man who pushes the button… As long as people imagine that someone is doing something to them and that they have no control, then they have no control."

'Happy Xmas (War Is Over)' was released in the USA on 1 December, to a disappointing response. In Britain the single was delayed for another year, held up by rumours of a publishing dispute over Yoko's co-credits. But when it did appear it went Top 5, appealing to the home market's partiality to seasonal singles. The song would enjoy the same recurring popularity as two other stocking fillers of the period, Slade's 'Merry Xmas Everybody' and Wizzard's 'I Wish It Could Be Christmas Every Day'. Rare indeed is the English pub jukebox that does not give all three hits an annual airing even today.

WOMAN IS THE NIGGER OF THE WORLD

Once ensconced in New York City, John became even more susceptible to feminist thinking, for this town had been the crucible of Women's Liberation since the late Sixties. A fine 1972 drawing by John, "New York Woman" depicts a naked African-American female, standing by Manhattan's skyscrapers, holding a plump, bald, cigar-smoking little man in the palm of her hand.

But of course his foremost tutor in the subject was Yoko, co-author of this song. "Woman Is The nigger Of The world," implying the universal nature of sexual inequality, was an aphorism of Yoko's, unveiled in a March 1969 profile of Yoko in the British women's magazine *Nova*. She later revealed that the idea was inspired by her first experiences with John. The Beatles, she considered, brought a new sensitivity to pop music, but in their private lives they remained four traditional Liverpool men. (John, for example, would always get to read the newspaper before she did.) John, for his part, acknowledged that Yoko was the first woman he had ever met who demanded parity with him — all the more audacious when he was a famous rock star. "But I'm King John of England!" was his attitude. Yoko, then, was the little boy who told the Emperor he was naked.

Recorded in March 1972, 'Woman Is the Nigger of the World' was issued as a single, preceding the *Some Time In New York City* album. Spector and the Elephant's Memory band bestowed the song with a strong performance, distinguished yet again by some magisterial saxophone, this time by Stan Bronstein. But John felt that his lyrics did not match the power of Yoko's title. Like several of his political songs, the verses have a second-hand quality, with John relaying received opinions. They lack the tang of individual artistry of, say, 'Strawberry Fields Forever'. Still, they are vivid, and effective enough at introducing

A Women's Liberation parade in New York, 1970. Introduced to feminism by Yoko, John responded with 'Woman Is the Nigger of the World'.

unfamiliar ideas into the mainstream.

Controversy was inevitable. A few feminist voices condemned the song for portraying women as weak and seemingly passive. Prior to John's debut of the song on Dick Cavett's TV show in May, the host apologised in advance for any offence it might give to middle America — although, as he wryly noted afterwards, most of the eventual complaints objected to his apology rather than to the song itself. In fact the media's chief difficulty with the single, as it turned out, was not the feminist content, but the incendiary word "nigger". Most radio stations steered clear of the record altogether.

To John's relief, black Congressman Ron Dellums issued a statement of support: "If you define 'nigger' as someone whose lifestyle is defined by others, whose opportunities are defined by others, whose role in society is defined by others, the good news is you don't have to be black to be a nigger in this society. Most of the people in America are niggers."

ATTICA STATE

On 9 October 1971, in a Syracuse, New York hotel, John held a party for his 31st birthday and the local opening of Yoko's new exhibition, *This Is Not Here*. The *Imagine* album had been released just 24 hours earlier. Revels that night included a six-hour jam session with guests such as Phil Spector, Ringo Starr and the poet Allen Ginsberg. John used the occasion to work up a new song commenting on the recent bloodbath at the Attica Correctional Facility in upstate New York. On 13 September a riot broke out in the prison after 1,200 inmates, mostly black, had taken 50 hostages and issued demands over conditions and terms for amnesty. The army and police went in shooting, killing 32 prisoners and 10 guards. John was among those who blamed the brutality of the authorities' response on state governor Nelson Rockefeller.

Though at pains to stress their sympathies lay with relatives of the guards as well, John and Yoko did make a surprise appearance at a benefit for the families of the dead prisoners, held at Harlem's Apollo Theatre on 17 December. Aretha Franklin was among the other artists who lent their support to the event. Meanwhile, life returned to normal in Attica State. Among its future inmates, come December 1980, would be one Mark Chapman.

The beat poet Allen Ginsberg was another New York comrade of John's, present at the writing of 'Attica State'.

New York state troops arriving on the morning of the final assault on Attica prison.

NANTUCKET

NEW YORK CITY

In 1980 Lennon described 'New York City' as "a bit of journalese." Virtually a sequel to 1969's 'The Ballad of John and Yoko', it's a straightforward diary of his recent adventures, but delivered with a boisterous drive that testifies to the new lease of life that the Big Apple had given him. He loved the feeling he could walk its streets unmolested, in a way that wasn't possible in London. (Just the reverse, in fact, of most people's impression of the two cities.) He makes passing reference to his problems with the immigration service, but replies, "the Statue of Liberty said 'Come!'".

Among the episodes recounted are his Fillmore concert with Frank Zappa, the Attica benefit at the Apollo and a visit to the New York rock club Max's Kansas City. There is also a description of his meeting with a local street musician, David Peel, whose favourite pitch was Washington Square Park. It was here, on the same day that he met Frank Zappa, that John stood in the crowd and heard Peel sing 'The Pope Smokes Dope' in tribute to Lennon and his criminal past. (The busker's own album was entitled *Have A Marijuana.*) Encouraged by his Yippie friend Jerry Rubin, he met Peel again the next week, jamming with him in the East Village and – to the delight of John's romantic rebel heart – getting moved on by the police.

John went on to produce Peel's album, *The Pope Smokes Dope*, releasing it through Apple. Lennon, Peel and Rubin announced they were "the Rock Liberation Front". And the FBI, preparing a dossier on John, actually pasted Peel's photo in their file by mistake.

A solid, rousing rocker, 'New York City' is the best defence witness in the case of *Some Time In New York City*. Elsewhere there are symptoms of John's lack of confidence in his new material, and it's likely Phil Spector was losing interest too. But Elephant's Memory, while by no means a versatile or subtle band, could storm superbly through a number such as this. John was attracted to their brassy sound because, most of all, it bore little resemblance to the Beatles.

New York City became Lennon's adopted home from 1971 to the end of his life. In the face of government efforts to deport him, John proclaimed his fervent wish to become a US resident.

SUNDAY BLOODY SUNDAY

On 11 August 1971, in one of John's last acts as a British resident, he joined a street demonstration in London, urging the government to pull its troops out of Northern Ireland. Since 1969 there had been renewed violence in this province of the United Kingdom, bitterly divided between its "Nationalist" Catholic minority (who wanted union with the Irish Republic) and the "Loyalist" Protestant majority, fiercely committed to the British link. Initially, troops were sent in to keep the warring factions apart, but the Catholics soon regarded them as an army of foreign occupation. Some Nationalists gave support to the newly-revived IRA.

Some six months later, on Sunday afternoon, 30 January 1972, about 10,000 people marched in the Catholic Bogside district of Derry. Targets of their protest included the new policy of internment, or imprisonment without trial for terrorist suspects. Fighting broke out and soldiers of the British Parachute Regiment opened fire, killing 13 civilians. The massacre was instantly dubbed "Bloody Sunday", in reference to a day of similar bloodshed back in 1920.

Lennon, by now in New York, was outraged by the news. His radical sympathies, combined with awareness of his own Irish roots, had disposed him towards the Nationalist cause. Within days he'd dashed off an angry song of response. Its title probably prompted by a 1971 John Schlesinger movie, *Sunday Bloody Sunday* rails against "Anglo pigs and Scotties" (the English had encouraged Scottish Protestants to settle in Ireland) and "concentration camps", and prays that the Falls Road, the Catholic area of Belfast, be "free forever".

Even Paul McCartney, always considered the less political of the pair, was moved to indignation. At almost the same moment that John was composing 'Sunday Bloody Sunday', Paul was in London recording 'Give Ireland Back to the Irish', with an atypically strident lyric that invokes his own Irish ancestry, albeit tempered by a statement of his British patriotism. It would be interesting to know if the two rivals were aware of each other's efforts at the time.

John explained that he wrote songs like 'Sunday Bloody Sunday' because he wanted to state his views as simply as rock'n'roll itself: "So now it's Awop bop a loobop, Get outta Ireland." He told his interviewer Roy Carr: "Here am I in New York and I hear about the 13 people shot dead in Ireland, and I react immediately. And being what I am, I react in four-to-the-bar with a guitar break in the middle… It's all over now. It's gone. My songs are not there to be digested and pulled apart like the Mona Lisa. If people on the street think about it, that's all there is to it."

There is a defensive note to John's comment. His disgust at the murder of innocent people was real enough, but topical punditry was not the equal of lasting art. Nor were simplistic choruses, however heartfelt, always adequate in the face of complex historical

▲ **British soldiers confront Irish nationalists in Derry on Bloody Sunday. Lennon was enraged by the killing of 13 of the protestors.**

problems. Over time, Lennon's 'Sunday Bloody Sunday' has been all but forgotten — displaced, since 1983, by U2's more thoughtful song of the same name.

THE LUCK OF THE IRISH

A few days after Bloody Sunday, on 5 February, Lennon joined Jerry Rubin and about 5,000 others in a protest outside the New York offices of the British airline BOAC. John weighed in with a rendition of 'The Luck Of The Irish', a song he'd written the previous November, and performed at Ann Arbor in December. For once, John was agreeably struck by police handling of a demo — most of those cops, he concluded, were Irish too.

In a speech to the multitudes, John stressed his own Irish heritage. Just as the song mentions Liverpool, so he explained his home town's unofficial status as "the capital of Ireland" due to the huge numbers who had emigrated there. But "the Irish question", as it was known to generations of perplexed English politicians, caused John deep misgivings. It was one thing to indulge a sentimental affinity with old-time republicanism, but another to endorse the new, hardline paramilitaries. In time, the Provisional IRA looked less like defenders of the ghetto and more like terror its. Essentially a liberal pacifist, John's interest was in Civil Rights rather than armed struggle.

Alas, 'The Luck Of The Irish' was a poor vehicle for any viewpoint. Simplistic polemic rubs shoulders with tourist brochure clichés ("Let's walk over rainbows like leprechauns") in a lame folk song pastiche, trilled in part by Yoko, which induces more embarrassment than enlightenment.

JOHN SINCLAIR

John Sinclair was a leading light of the American Sixties counter culture. A left wing author and former beat poet, he was manager of the confrontational Detroit rock band MC5 and political organiser of the White Panther party, a student/hippie equivalent of the ghetto-based Black Panther movement. He liked to summarise his manifesto as "rock and roll and dope and fucking in the streets".

If the Vietnam war was a rallying point for opposition groups, then official repression of the underground lifestyle — drugs in particular — fuelled youthful dissent even further. By 1970 the worsening climate drove a section of the Woodstock generation into more committed forms of militancy. For his pains, Sinclair received a savage ten-year jail sentence for passing two marijuana joints to an undercover narcotics agent. Remembering his own marijuana conviction in England in 1968, Lennon saw John Sinclair's fate as more evidence of the establishment using the drug laws to hound its enemies.

Radical writer John Sinclair: Lennon campaigned to get him released from prison.

On 10 December 1971, John and Yoko made a guest appearance at a pro-Sinclair rally in Ann Arbor, Michigan. Among the numbers he played at the event was 'The Luck of the Irish' and, specially written for the event, 'John Sinclair'. To everyone's amazement, the authorities released Sinclair three days later, just 27 months into his sentence. Their move was prompted by recent changes in drug legislation but they were also aware, no doubt, that the issue was becoming a *cause célèbre*. Rarely, if ever, had a protest song appeared to achieve change at such dramatic speed. Free at last, Sinclair placed a call to John in New York, thanking him for his contribution.

Though it's no classic, John's song has a compelling urgency about it, and some pungent lyrics about the CIA's involvement in drug-trafficking in Asia. What the verses lack in elegance, they make up for in honest anger. The Ann Arbor concert inspired him to plan a nationwide protest tour — he hoped to get Bob Dylan on board, too — that would culminate outside the Republican Party's National Convention. It never came to pass, but the rumours did nothing to soften the administration's dislike of Lennon, and they redoubled their efforts to get him expelled.

The MC5 were one vehicle for their manager John Sinclair's manifesto: "Rock and roll and dope and fucking in the streets."

ANGELA

The jailing of Black Panther, Angela Davis, gave John a subject for another protest song.

Ever observant of Dylan's progress, John was impressed by Bob's return to social commentary in the form of a November 1971 single, 'George Jackson'. In it, Dylan laments the killing of Jackson, a Black Panther being held at San Quentin Prison on a one year-to-life sentence for robbery. A year earlier, some Jackson supporters had taken hostages at the Marin County Courthouse in a bid to get him freed, but the attempt failed in a fatal shoot-out. Another Black Panther, UCLA lecturer Angela Davis, was charged with kidnapping, conspiracy and murder for having helped the hostage-takers. After spending a year on the run, she was captured in late 1970. But Jackson himself was shot in August 1971 following an "escape bid" which some suspected was a frame-up.

Now John was approached by friends of the imprisoned Davis and asked to contribute a song to the campaign for her release. The resulting 'Angela' is largely sung by Yoko and does not rank among the couple's best collaborations. It may, indeed, be one of their worst, on a record which offers some formidable contenders for that title. It was also completely upstaged by Mick Jagger's own Davis tribute, 'Sweet Black Angel', on the Rolling Stones' epochal *Exile On Main Street* album.

The comparison is telling, because rock music was no longer led by Beatles or by ex-Beatles. It was left to their Sixties contemporaries the Stones to make the definitive rock album of the early Seventies. Simultaneously, the American heartland was falling for a younger British band, Led Zeppelin. Britain had found its "new Beatles" in T. Rex, while another newcomer, David Bowie, was recording his groundbreaking *Ziggy Stardust*. One way or another, while John was making *Some Time In New York City*, the future was being made without him. His overtly political music had brought him very little reward, either creatively or commercially. In search of fresh inspiration, he would have to turn inwards once more.

The trouble was, at first sight, there seemed to be nothing left in there.

MIND GAMES

5

ALBUM

MIND GAMES
'Mind Games'
'Tight A$'
'Aisumasen (I'm Sorry)'
'One Day (At A Time)'
'Bring On The Lucie (Freda Peeple)'
'Nutopian International Anthem'
'Intuition'
'Out The Blue'
'Only People'
'I Know (I Know)'
'You Are Here'
'Meat City'

The Dakota became John's home in 1973.

The Lennons at the One to One benefit in Madison Square, August 1972. That night's show was John's last complete concert.

The story of Lennon's Seventies is, in retrospect, strewn with fateful landmarks. On 30 August 1972, for example, when he played two shows with Elephant's Memory at Madison Square Garden, he was performing what turned out to be the last full concerts of his life.

Happily they were good ones, raising funds for the handicapped children's charity One To One. Such a public-spirited gesture may have been John's way to improve his image in the eyes of officialdom. At the same time, however, the paramilitary duds he wore on stage were a reminder that he was still a fighter of sorts, and not the beatific peacenik of former years.

Meanwhile, in his war with the US immigration service, John won testimonials from many Americans: just a few include Norman Mailer, Fred Astaire, Kurt Vonnegut and Tony Curtis. The *New York Post* said, "He has improved this town just by showing up." The deportation hearings even got a handwritten letter from Bob Dylan: "John and Yoko add a great voice and drive to this country's so called ART INSTITUTION. They inspire and transcend and stimulate and by doing so, only help others to see pure light and in doing that, put an end to this mild dull taste of petty commercialism which is being passed off as artist art by the overpowering mass media. Hurray for John and Yoko. Let them stay and live here and breathe."

John's own view was sardonic: "It keeps the conservatives happy that they're doing something about me, and what I represent. And it keeps the liberals happy, because I haven't actually been thrown out. So everybody's happy." His prospects were briefly improved when news arrived from England of the arrest of Scotland Yard's Sergeant Pilcher. The man responsible for John's 1968 marijuana bust was now on trial himself, charged with "conspiracy to pervert the course of justice," casting some doubt over the validity of John's original conviction.

Whether it was mere expediency or some deeper shift in his thinking, Lennon now presented a more acceptable face to the authorities by suddenly dumping a lot of his radical baggage. On the advice of his lawyers, plans were abandoned for the nationwide anti-war tour. The protest songs tailed off. He grew tired of his Yippie allies — having secured a slot for them on *The Mike Douglas Show*, he was appalled that "none of them knew how to talk to the people — let alone lead them." Characters like Rubin, Hoffman and David Peel dropped out of the picture. Peel has since talked of the Cinderella effect felt by the friends of celebrities. In their company you are a kind of prince, made radiant by the reflected fame. But when midnight arrives, your limousine becomes a pumpkin. You're alone once more and back in your rags.

The wider climate was changing, too. By 1973 the Sixties' Woodstock Nation was a faded dream, and "Me Decade" was kicking in, alongside a global recession. And Lennon's old nemesis Richard Nixon was on the ropes. On 27 June John travelled to Washington to watch the Watergate hearings. On the same visit he joined a demonstration outside the South Vietnamese embassy, but even the war would soon subside, taking with it the chief rallying point for dissenters.

There was symbolism, too, in his April 1973 move to the Dakota Building on 72nd Street. He'd forsaken funky downtown Greenwich Village for an uptown celebrity bolt-hole. The Dakota, which has been Yoko's home ever since, was a luxury apartment block, built in 1888, whose gothic gauntness made it the setting for *Rosemary's Baby*. From John's new windows he could overlook the lushness of Central Park — modelled, as it happened, on a humbler Victorian expanse back in his native Liverpool.

Another change was in the air. There were rumours of a rift between John and Yoko. While he idled away his time, she was much busier, releasing her *Approximately Infinite Universe* album to better reviews (though inevitably even poorer sales) than *Some Time In New York City*. Perhaps they really did work better apart.

When John eventually roused himself to make another album, as his contract demanded, he seemed dispirited. Early in 1973 a DJ asked him how the new music was shaping up. "It's getting to be work," came his slack response. "It's ruining the music. It's like after

John and Yoko attended the Watergate hearings in Washington on 27 June 1973, confirming their worst suspicions of the Nixon administration.

At a New York peace rally in May 1972: the *Mind Games* album saw John turn away from such overt campaigning.

you leave school and you don't want to read a book. Every time I strap the guitar on, it's the same old jazz. I just feel like breathing a bit."

Sessions began in August, at New York's Record Plant, with John producing. His chosen guitarist was a local session ace, David Spinozza, who had played on McCartney's hated *Ram* album two years earlier. (His co-player on that record, Hugh McCracken, would later become John's guitarist on *Double Fantasy*.) Released in October, the *Mind Games* album was an often flaccid album whose chief claim on public favour was that it wasn't *Some Time In New York City*. He'd successfully shrugged off the ranting image, but his private life was unravelling and the strain of his constant fight against deportation was beginning to wear him down.

Embarrassingly for John, *Mind Games* was outpaced in the charts by Ringo's new album, released the same day. Even worse, he was thoroughly eclipsed a month later when Paul McCartney hit peak solo form with his Number 1 success *Band On The Run*. Called upon to promote his record, John could not muster much enthusiasm: "It's just an album," he shrugged. "It's rock'n'roll at different speeds. There's no very deep message about it. The only reason I make albums is because you're supposed to."

Observe the vinyl version of *Mind Games*' artwork and there is an interesting quirk. Against Bob Gruen's photo of Yoko as a mountain range, a blurred Lennon steps across the plain. On the reverse he is larger and closer. According to John's new friend May Pang, he described this as himself "walking away from Yoko". By the time of the record's release, he and his wife were living on opposite coasts of the United States.

MIND GAMES

The older John became the more he turned to books for the information that his hungry mind required. Janov's *The Primal Scream*, indeed, had sparked off the enthusiasm that produced an entire album of material. Mind Games' title track was itself named after a book, this time a psychological tract by Robert Masters and Jean Houston that tapped into the post-hippie theme of consciousness raising. After the relative harshness of the *Some Time In New York City* songs, 'Mind Games' reflected a more meditative Lennon, guitars overdubbed into a quasi-orchestral lushness that marked a partial return to *Imagine* territory. We're back on familiar ground as John prescribes a global projection of the power of love.

While 'Mind Games' proved to be one of the more popular late Lennon compositions, it's arguable that the song would have been even greater, had

John stuck to his first idea and called it 'Make Love, Not War'. This was its original chorus, and there is a tantalising remnant at the song's fade, where John sings "I want you to make love, not war," in place of the "Mind games forever" refrain. He'd abandoned the plan, feeling that by 1973 the slogan's hour had passed, and that people would now regard it as a cliché ("I know you've heard it before," he adds at the very end). But, cliché or not, "make love not war" might have had more lasting impact. It certainly carries more emotive weight than the dated psycho-jargon of its replacement.

'Mind Games', then, is the anthem that never was. Still it contains some enjoyable imagery, notably the "druid dudes" and "mind guerillas" exercising their cosmic powers in mankind's quest for enlightenment. The song's chief significance lies in its mystical atmosphere — an abrupt signal of John's loss of interest in orthodox political agendas.

He liked to say that its middle-eight section ("Love is the answer" etc) was reggae-derived, though neither he nor his musicians were used to the style at that time.

Country rockers the Flying Burrito Brothers: pedal steel player Pete Kleinow was one of John's most talented collaborators.

TIGHT A$

The second song was worrying evidence that everything John had to say — and it was little enough — he'd already said on *Mind Games*' opening track. All the musicianly talent assembled for these sessions could not disguise the slightness of 'Tight A$', although the country-rock star "Sneaky" Pete Kleinow, of Gram Parsons' Flying Burrito Brothers, contributes some scintillating pedal-steel guitar. Essentially, the song was John's tribute to New York's hard-living, hard-playing ethos, but the city's energy is hardly captured here. The fact was that John's inner exhaustion was beginning to tell. He was falling back on his old facility for puns, and knocking off songs to fulfil the album's quota rather than for their own sake.

AISUMASEN (I'M SORRY)

John had been toying with this tune since 1971, when its working title was 'Call My Name'. In its finished form, however, it is John who is calling Yoko's name, thus inverting his role from comforter to supplicant. This meekly submissive tone would soon become a staple feature of his songwriting, with numerous examples to follow. It's extremely revealing that one of the few fragments of Japanese that John had so far mastered was "Aisumasen" — "I'm sorry".

It's unknown whether he was apologising for any specific incident, but a favourite candidate must be the US election night of 7 November 1972 when John, Yoko and radical friends watched the TV in dismay while Richard Nixon chalked up a landslide victory over his liberal Democratic opponent George McGovern. Political disillusionment hit John hard that evening; hopes of an end to his visa problems took a knock as well. Worst of all, it was rumoured that John humiliated Yoko by openly seducing another woman at the party. Whatever the exact origins of 'Aisumasen', its weak tone compares unfavourably with 'Jealous Guy' and did much to cement the image of Yoko as John's domineering dragon lady.

A jubilant Nixon celebrates his second-term victory in November 1972. Lennon was demoralised by the result.

ONE DAY (AT A TIME)

In the vacuum caused by John's loss of political faith, the nature of his partnership with Yoko assumes centre stage in *Mind Games*. The duality of their relationship is captured at the outset of this song, when John describes her as being both his weakness and his strength.

Unfortunately, perhaps, it is the element of weakness which seems to predominate here. The very title, borrowed from the language of recovering alcoholics, betrays an unhealthy streak of dependency on Lennon's part, with little indication that the condition might be mutual. "Mrs Lennon" was tired of her passive public role. On the next album, *Walls And Bridges*, the full extent of John's predicament would be made apparent.

The arrangement, too, with its echoes of old-fashioned Tin Pan Alley hackery, reminds us that John was not above the facile, lightweight style that he used to scorn in Paul McCartney. The track captures Lennon in a rare period of aimlessness.

BRING ON THE LUCIE (FREDA PEEPLE)

John recovered some of his rock'n'roll bite, as well as radical indignation, on this stomping condemnation of the Nixon administration, who stand accused of war-mongering abroad and corruption at home. Only a passing accusation that the enemy's name is "666" — Biblical code for the Antichrist, and Lennon's nickname for Nixon — marks it as a *Mind Games* song instead of one from its predecessor. As John put it later, "It was Bell, Book and Candle against Mr 666 Nixon. We used magic, prayer and children to fight the good fight." There is more punning in the song title, and a reassuring flash of Lennon wit in the track's intro, when he urges his band "over the hill", in the manner of a war-movie sergeant to his platoon. Once again, though, thanks are due to "Sneaky" Pete's keening pedal steel, and to Jim Keltner's galumphing drums, for hauling John's track above the mediocre.

The English saint and statesman, Thomas More, whose ideal land Utopia was echoed in John's dream of "Nutopia".

NUTOPIAN INTERNATIONAL ANTHEM

On 1 April 1973, All Fools' Day, John and Yoko called a press conference at which they were expected to discuss their deportation fight. To widespread bemusement, however, they chose the occasion to unveil nothing less than a new nation. This "Declaration of Nutopia" appears on the *Mind Games* album sleeve: "We announce the birth of a conceptual country, NUTOPIA. Citizenship of the country can be obtained by declaration of your awareness of NUTOPIA. NUTOPIA has no land, no boundaries, no passports, only people. NUTOPIA has no laws other than cosmic. All people of NUTOPIA are ambassadors of the country. As two ambassadors of NUTOPIA, we ask for diplomatic immunity and recognition in the United Nations of our country and its people."

The original *Utopia* was a book published in 1516 by Sir Thomas More, an English chancellor beheaded by King Henry VIII for remaining loyal to the Pope. (More was declared a saint by the Catholic Church in 1935, 400 years after his death.) Just as More attacked inequitable social and economic conditions and described an imaginary, ideal commonwealth based on reason, so John Lennon's "new Utopia" represented a fantasy world, like that of 'Imagine', where our freedoms are not confined by national divisions. Given his immigration problems, John's satirical intentions were obvious. Nevertheless, his lawyers felt it best to carry on contesting the case through the courts.

It really comes as no surprise that John's 'Nutopian International Anthem' turns out to be a few seconds of complete silence. The name of Sir Thomas More's imaginary happy land came from ancient Greek, meaning "Nowhere". In asserting his Nutopian citizenship, therefore, John at last became "a real Nowhere Man."

Having failed to seize the public imagination to even the smallest degree, "Nutopia" was never heard of again, while Lennon himself was forced to continue wondering where he would be living in few months' time. The uncertainty was just one more destabilizing factor at work in his life.

INTUITION

In a figure less likeable than Lennon, 'Intuition' would be very annoying indeed. Set to a cloying, bouncy melody, it's a number that catches John on a good day, celebrating his supposed talent for making the best of life and — just a little smugly — implying we could all do worse than to follow his example. John may well have been right to trust his instincts — they may not be rational, he implies, but they have a wisdom of their own — but his better songs acknowledged the darkness and the turbulence of his inner life, as this disposable ditty so lamentably fails to do. As a skip-along lilt, it's poor. As a recipe for psychic sunshine, it's a case of "the blind leading the blind".

John and Yoko, full of the joys of Spring, in Central Park in 1973, on a househunting trip to view apartments in the Dakota Building.

OUT THE BLUE

One of John's many songs of devotion to Yoko, 'Out The Blue' boasts a heavenly choir in the background, but otherwise confines itself to a modest statement of gratitude. John expresses a sense of wonder at Yoko's unforeseen arrival in his life, "out [of] the blue". Years later he described his recurrent yearning for a fantasy soul mate: "Someone that I had already known, but somehow had lost." At first he pictured this ideal woman as dark-haired, with high cheekbones, a "free-spirited artist" in the style of French actress Juliette Greco. In time his allegiance switched to Brigitte Bardot (he even persuaded his first wife Cynthia to imitate the blonde goddess's look). But in Yoko, John felt he'd finally found the embodiment of his original vision. For all her virtues, Cynthia was a conventional choice of wife for John, whereas her successor — an assertive, avant garde Japanese artist — was the partner that people least expected. She came, in all her strangeness, "like a UFO". Out of the blue.

ONLY PEOPLE

The germ of this jolly, inconsequential rocker is in Yoko Ono's pronouncement, quoted on the album sleeve, that "Only people can change the world." John couples it with a less portentous aphorism of his own, "Madness is the first sign of dandruff." One wonders if the latter line might have made a better song. As it stands, 'Only People' revisits the general thought behind 'Instant Karma!' — namely our collective potential for shaping the future — but without that song's joyful confidence. It's questionable whether John was repeating his theme because he believed in mantra-like repetition, or because he was running out of fresh ideas. Various forces were at work, in that summer of 1973, to hasten Nixon's downfall — he finally resigned one year later — but a crowd in New York's Record Plant, chanting "We don't want no pig brother scene!" was probably not among them.

John's ideal woman was "a free spirited artist". Before Yoko, his fantasy had turned on French actress Juliette Greco.

Bigots attacked the Lennons for their mixed-race marriage. John thought of seeking advice from British jazz artists Cleo Laine and Johnny Dankworth.

YOU ARE HERE

John presents his romance with Yoko in a global light, portraying their relationship as the union of Liverpool and Tokyo, or a symbolic marriage of the hemispheres. In the final verse he contradicts a quotation from the patriotic English poet Rudyard Kipling, "East is East and West is West and never the twain shall meet." Prejudice against foreigners such as Yoko helped to turn John against his homeland, and to seek sanctuary in the more cosmopolitan life of New York City. "It was humiliating and painful for both if us," he recalled. "I was ashamed of Britain."

The title for 'You Are Here' came from a "conceptual" exhibition that John staged in London in 1968. The centrepiece of *You Are Here* was a circular white screen, on which he'd written those three words for anyone who cared to inspect them. He then released 365 helium balloons from the event, with reply cards attached, to be found by random members of the British public. Of more than 100 cards returned, John was dismayed to find that many expressed contempt for his recent eccentricities and his new Japanese girlfriend. He took a morbid fascination in the racialist hate-mail he received, and even considered getting it published. He also thought of asking advice from the London jazz musicians Johnny Dankworth and Cleo Laine, who were themselves a mixed-race couple. Residual anti-Japanese feeling was an unfortunate feature of post-War Britain, and remarkable in that it actually exceeded any lingering hostility to the Germans.

The issue of inter-racial marriage was clearly important to John, but his strong feelings did not inspire a vivid song in 'You Are Here'. Its imagery is hackneyed ("Three thousand light years from the land of the rising sun") while the musical exotica is trite — it would be a few more years until John began listening seriously to Japanese music, and he never got the chance to make meaningful use of it in his own music.

Strangely, the track begins with John grunting "Nine". The number was of peculiar significance to him, as we shall see.

I KNOW (I KNOW)

With a finger-picked guitar pattern reminiscent of the Beatles, 'I Know (I Know)' is one of John's stronger ballads in this set, although its lyric ploughs what was rapidly becoming a familiar furrow. Once more, then, he plights his troth to Yoko, while also pausing to apologise for his unworthiness. But the evidence is that his wife remained unmoved. Before the record had even appeared in the shops, John was living apart from Yoko — apparently at her request.

MEAT CITY

Much as he railed against its politicians, John was deeply excited by America — after all, it was the birthplace of his beloved rock'n'roll — and 'Meat City' captures that excitement wonderfully. The song began to take shape almost as soon as he arrived in New York City to live. At first it was a boogie called 'Shoeshine', but grew from a simple celebration of the music into a powerful account of his pilgrimage: "I been to the mountain to see for myself." He may be appalled or bewildered by some of the sights that greet him in the madness of the city, but he exults in its vitality. In John's mind, his early infatuation with Elvis Presley and Chuck Berry was a prelude to his life. America was where he should have been born, and the land where he was destined to live.

Then he turns his thoughts to China, a land as far away and other-worldly as America itself had once seemed. John saw China as the next frontier. "I shall go there," he declared in 1972. "I will take the opportunity to try to see Mao. If he is ill or dead or refuses to see me, too bad. But if I go there I want to meet people who are doing something important. I want to take a rock band to China. That is really what I want to do. To play rock in China. They have yet to see that." In the low-key travels of his final years, John did get to visit Hong Kong — but China's communist mainland remained off-limits to the average rock'n'roll tour.

The title of the song may have come to John from a popular cartoon poster of the time, showing a mother pig and her offspring, chatting complacently while they're trucked towards their fatal destination, "Meat City". The porcine theme is underscored by shouts of "Pig meat city" and, reportedly, by a backwards message: the inverted vocal interlude has been deciphered as "Fuck a pig."

The last track on the album, 'Meat City' presents a satisfying opposite to the opening number — earthy and physical where 'Mind Games' is ethereal and contemplative. These two extremes would continue doing battle inside John Lennon's life and work. But, for the next few years, it would be his 'Meat City' side that emerged on top — with almost catastrophic consequences.

Chairman Mao Tse Tung: Lennon never fulfilled his ambitions to meet the Communist leader or to bring rock'n'roll to China.

16 WALLS AND BRIDGES

In 1973 John went haywire. As he later put it to BBC interviewer Andy Peebles, "The feminist side of me died slightly." May Pang was a New York-Chinese girl who had worked for the Lennons and their manager Allen Klein since 1969. When John and Yoko moved into the Dakota building, May became their in-house assistant and, at Yoko's instigation (according to May Pang's account, at least), began an affair with him. So commenced the most bizarre interlude in Lennon's extraordinary life, the legendary "Lost Weekend".

Yoko promotes the view that she banished John from the Dakota in order to confront his demons, to return only when she deemed him ready. "She don't suffer fools gladly," said John in 1980, "even if she's married to him." Tiring of him, and of her role as "Mrs Lennon", Yoko was ready to assert herself. For his own part, John seemed keen to escape. He quickly fell for May, and the pair soon hit Los Angeles like eloping runaways, staying at a variety of addresses.

Whatever its cause, this lost weekend was an almighty bender, a 15-month rampage. Suddenly off the leash, John was a born again Rock Pig, running free across LA on a binge of drink and general boorishness. In later years, reunited with Yoko, he was careful not to call it a period of liberation. In fact his 1980 view was, "I was like an elephant in a zoo, aware that it's trapped but not able to get out." Though in exile, he would still make or receive up to 20 calls a day to and from Yoko at the Dakota.

May Pang was undoubtedly a comfort to him, but he also needed a new sort of stability — something to restore his artistic focus and give him direction. Instead, what he got was Phil Spector and a gang of good ol' boys that starred Keith Moon, Harry Nilsson and Ringo Starr. It was Brandy Alexanders all round.

Spector and Lennon concocted a plan for an LP of rock'n'roll cover versions, which would re-invigorate John with a blast of back-to-basics Fifties fundamentalism. Spector would once again be his saviour. And the project had a second advantage. John had just been accused of plagiarism by an opportunist music publisher called Morris Levy — a veteran Tin Pan Alley hustler who had once attempted to copyright the term "rock'n'roll" itself. Levy owned Chuck Berry's song 'You Can't Catch Me', briefly pastiched on 'Come Together' from the Beatles' *Abbey Road*. To forestall a lawsuit, John promised to record three other Levy copyrights on his next album.

But the *Rock'N'Roll* sessions at A&M's LA studios were an all-star nightmare of drunken disorganisation, punctuated by the odd gunshot. Deafened by his pistol-toting producer's prank, John said, "Phil, if you're going to kill me, kill me. But don't fuck with my ears. I need 'em." Spector was gifted at orchestrating sonic excess, but these recordings were a mess. Scores of eminent players such as Leon Russell, Dr John and Charlie Watts were hired, playing their parts over and over. But the chaotic self-indulgence and chronic indecision proved too much. Evicted from A&M, the team decamped to Record Plant West with scarcely improved results. Then Spector disappeared with the tapes and the whole unhappy project was shelved. To compound John's misery, *Mind Games* went on sale that month, to universal apathy.

Meanwhile John himself was going off the rails. The night he arrived at Ann Peebles' Troubadour show, sporting a sanitary towel on his head, is merely the most notorious in a string of sordid incidents. In 1974 he claimed the stories of depravity were "mostly fiction, with a grain of alcohol," but as he admitted at the time, "I've never drunk so much in my life." Identifying the source of his desolation, he admitted, "I get my daily Yoko out of a bottle these days." In March 1974 he was back at the Troubadour, brawling with anyone who stopped him and heckling that night's act, The Smothers Brothers — a bitter moment for Tommy Smothers, who'd strummed guitar at John's side during 'Give Peace A Chance'. When he hit a waitress, she remarked, "It's not the pain that hurts, it's finding out that one of your idols is a real asshole."

With *Rock'N'Roll* on hold, John agreed to produce Harry Nilsson's new album *Pussy Cats*. Sessions began in LA, until John decided it would be better for everyone's health and sanity if they switched to New York. With May Pang he found a penthouse apartment on East 52nd Street, a little way up from the United Nations building. Once the Nilsson project was completed, John began his own climb back from artistic decrepitude by starting an all-new album, *Walls And Bridges*. There was a further distraction in July, when

ALBUMS

WALLS AND BRIDGES
'Going Down On Love'
'Whatever Gets You Thru The Night'
'Old Dirt Road'
'What You Got'
'Bless You'
'Scared'
'#9 Dream'
'Surprise Surprise (Sweet Bird Of Paradox)'
'Steel And Glass'
'Beef Jerky'
'Nobody Loves You (When You're Down And Out)'

ROCK'N'ROLL

In March, 1974, during the depths of his "lost weekend", John has a drunken scuffle at the Troubadour Club in LA. Behind him is his ever-present accomplice Harry Nilsson.

John with his assistant May Pang, the woman who became his lover during the year-long separation from Yoko.

the government issued a new ultimatum, giving him 60 days to leave the country. He commented at the time, "I can't leave here or they'd do a Charlie Chaplin on me and I don't want an award at 60 telling me how wonderful I used to be, but not quite wonderful enough to be allowed to live here now."

Of the *Walls And Bridges* title, John said only that it was "sent from above in the guise of a public service announcement," but it chimes nicely with the music's constant theme of barriers between him and Yoko. Whatever pain he was in, it inspired a great album. Released on 4 October 1974, the record also gave him a precious Number 1 hit in 'Whatever Gets You Thru The Night'. The *Walls And Bridges* sleeve was adorned by paintings he'd produced as a child, and carried a genealogical tract on the Irish origins of his surname.

There was also this cryptic message: "On 23 August 1974 at 9 o'clock I saw a UFO." The number nine held mystic significance for him, but of the sighting itself he said, "I went to the window, just dreaming around in my usual poetic frame of mind... hovering over the building, no more than a hundred feet away was this thing with ordinary electric light bulbs flashing on and off round the bottom, one non-blinking red light on top... What the Nixon is that?"

But John was not a fan of *Walls And Bridges*. "The only thing about it is it's new" was the best he could

say on its behalf. By 1980 he was ready to disown it entirely, calling it the work of "a semi-sick craftsman… There's no inspiration and there's misery. It gives off an aura of misery."

As recording began, the tapes of his abortive *Rock'N'Roll* sessions suddenly arrived from Phil Spector. Once *Walls And Bridges* was completed, John returned to them and used his new team of musicians to complete the project. From such unpromising origins, he fashioned a very respectable album. He nicknamed it "Old Hat", but *Rock'N'Roll* turned out to be a sophisticated take on the music of his adolescence. Both affectionate and distanced, he closed the record with a mock show business voice over, signing off from Record Plant East. He later guessed he'd meant the farewell with unconscious seriousness, because he did not record again for another five years.

As to the "lost weekend", which ended in his return to Yoko and the Dakota, May Pang disputes that it was "lost" at all. In that time he made some of the finest music of his whole career.

GOING DOWN ON LOVE

In a restrained but deeply felt performance, John raises the curtain on *Walls And Bridges* with a song that could practically be sub-titled 'The Ballad Of The Lost Weekend'. He mourns the loss of love, laments his own descent into aimless pleasure-seeking, and cries out for help. As an album, *Walls And Bridges* never deviates from the path indicated by 'Going Down On Love'. The record amounts to Lennon's *De Profundis* — a long, piteous call for Yoko to haul him out of this abyss. It's a melancholy note to open on: "Nothing doin' nowhere...". The irony is that in creative terms, there is more happening on *Walls And Bridges* than on records John made before and after, when he was in a happier frame of mind.

WHATEVER GETS YOU THRU THE NIGHT

John duets with Elton John at Madison Square Garden, 28 November, 1974 — the last time he appeared on a public stage.

During his separation from Yoko, John's new habit of socialising with fellow musicians had some dire consequences. One of the more fruitful acquaintances, however, was with Elton John, by now the most successful English pop star of the day. Lennon played Elton a tape of his new songs, inviting him to supply piano and backing vocals on any track he liked. Rather to John's disappointment, his guest plumped for Lennon's "least favourite" number, feeling it gave him the most space to contribute something extra. 'Whatever Gets You Thru The Night' turned out to be a lyrically slight but sonically storming rocker, that would give John his first solo Number 1 hit.

John had his doubts about the song, a vague ode to self-preservation that echoed his own insecurity and loss of direction. (He took the title from a line he'd heard on a TV programme about alcoholism.) But, in 1974, Elton's commercial instincts were keener than John's, and he reckoned the track was a sure-fire success. If it reached the top of the charts, he challenged, then John should repay the favour by appearing at one of Elton's live shows. 'Whatever Gets You Thru The Night', helped in large measure by Bobby Keyes' gusting tenor sax, duly became the US Number 1 on 16 November 1974, and John was honour-bound to show up at Elton John's concert at Madison Square Garden on Thanksgiving Day, the 28th of that month.

The gig was to have a double significance in John's life. At the after-show party in New York's Pierre Hotel, he began his reconciliation with Yoko. Less happily, it was also John's last ever appearance on a public stage. He joined Elton for versions of 'Whatever Gets You Thru The Night', 'Lucy In The Sky With Diamonds' and — poignantly, for his final song before a live audience — the McCartney number which had kicked off the first Beatles LP 11 years earlier, 'I Saw Her Standing There'. John dedicated it to "an old estranged fiancé of mine called Paul."

Pleased as he was by the popularity of 'Whatever Gets You Thru The Night' — a song that virtually resurrected his career — John never cared for it too much. "We didn't get a good take on the musicians," he reflected in 1980. He even went so far as to remark, half seriously, that it should have got to Number 39, not Number 1.

OLD DIRT ROAD

Laced with a high and lonesome guitar wail by Jesse Ed Davis, 'Old Dirt Road' carries backing vocals by Harry Nilsson, who co-wrote the song with John during their sessions for the *Pussy Cats* album. Foremost among his "lost weekend" partners in crime, Nilsson was a singer and songwriter so admired by John's old band that they used to call him "the Beatle across the water".

By 1980 Lennon was inclined to belittle his work from this period, and dismissed the number as a product of his and Nilsson's drunken sojourn. "It's just a song, you know," he told *Playboy*. "Well, seeing we're stuck in this bottle of vodka, we might as well try and do something." But it deserves a better

▲ Harry Nilsson took a walk on the wild side with Lennon in 1974: "Get one Beatle drunk and see what happens!"

appraisal than that. A possible descendant of the old Charlie Patton blues song 'Ain't Goin' Down That Dirt Road', resurrected by Howlin' Wolf in his 1970 London sessions with Eric Clapton, this Lennon/Nilsson collaboration has a drifting sadness that is truly affecting.

John's murder was to hit his old drinking buddy harder than most. In the decade up to his own death in January 1994, Harry Nilsson played an active role in America's Coalition To Stop Gun Violence. By that time, Nilsson had lived to rue his involvement in John's wild holiday. He felt that blame for incidents such as the Troubadour scuffles was often laid at his door. "That incident ruined my reputation for ten years," he said. "Get one Beatle drunk and see what happens!" John himself had protested, "So I was drunk. When it's Errol Flynn the showbiz writers say, 'Those were the days, when men were men.' When I do it, I'm a bum."

WHAT YOU GOT

There is a forceful current of emotion running through *Walls And Bridges* that sometimes outstrips John's powers of invention. In cursing his separation from Yoko, he cannot offer much more here than the stock phrase "You don't know what you got, until you lose it." He quotes the Little Richard rocker, 'Rip It Up' (reprised at the *Rock'N'Roll* sessions a few months later) when he declares that "it's Saturday night"; but this time he is not celebrating the fact so much as, perhaps, charting all the weeks that he's squandered in drinking to forget. Still, he screams the words at full throttle, while the band attempt a tough, rubbery take on Seventies funk. 'What You Got' is admittedly short on poetry, but it's satisfyingly stuffed with drama.

BLESS YOU

Being absent from its making, Yoko becomes more present on *Walls And Bridges* than any Lennon album she actually participated in. With its vaguely oriental shimmer, 'Bless You' invokes her most romantically. A ballad as fine as any he ever wrote, its lyric has John relaying his tenderest good wishes to the departed partner and whatever new lover she may have found. As such, it stands in total contrast to the 'Jealous Guy' school of Lennon songs — there is no suggestion here that he would rather see her dead than with another man. And yet, if he has found the strength and maturity to accept her independence, he does not relinquish his love.

At the Statue of Liberty on 30 October, 1974, in a shot that symbolised his battle with the US immigration service.

The final message of 'Bless You' is that he and Yoko remain spiritually connected. Their love transcends their physical separation.

In fact Yoko was not alone during John's "lost weekend". During sessions for the previous album *Mind Games*, she had grown fond of their star guitarist David Spinozza, around the same time that John was beginning his affair with May Pang. If John felt any misgivings about his wife's affection for Spinozza, he'd at least acquired sufficient maturity to compose a song as noble as 'Bless You'. Had the track appeared on, say, *Imagine*, it would be better recognised today. But, since all Lennon's best work was drawn from the well of his own experiences, 'Bless You' had to wait until he hit the emotional wastelands of 1974.

Though it's a little known Lennon number, there is evidence that the song found favour with its intended target, an audience of one. It's not surprising that 'Bless You' was one of the compositions that Yoko chose to include on the *Menlove Avenue* album, a 1986 compilation of John's demo tracks and unreleased recordings from the mid-Seventies. When he'd first played 'Bless You' to May Pang, she reassured him that Yoko would receive the tribute in the right spirit. "It's a beautiful song," she told him. "She's going to love it."

Lennon wondered if his song 'Scared' was an influence on the Rolling Stones' 'Miss You'. He later complained about Mick Jagger's criticism of his inactivity.

SCARED

In a significant touch, the brooding 'Scared' opens with the howl of a lone wolf. On the one hand, John is a timid traveller in the moonlit wilderness. On the other, he's a sort of werewolf himself, possessed by urges he cannot quite control. The song is manacled to an ominous marching beat, tramping forward like a prisoner to the gallows. In all, it seethes with underlying tension and dread inevitability.

John described 'Scared' as a summary of his feelings when away from Yoko, as the gloom descended and he was mired by an awful helplessness. In this predicament, he sings, "no bell, book or candle" can help him. This picturesque term for religion was a favourite phrase of his, taken from Shakespeare's *King John*: "Bell, book and candle shall not drive me back/When gold and silver becks me to come on." Homeless and uprooted, he next borrows Bob Dylan's line and describes himself as being "like a rolling stone." Coincidentally, Lennon later wondered if Mick Jagger had been listening to 'Scared' when he wrote the Rolling Stones' disco-flavoured 1978 hit 'Some Girls'. True, there are some parallels in the lyrics' theme of arid isolation, but the influence is far from obvious.

John himself saw 'Scared' as a confession of his private terror, in the same tradition as 'Help!'. He confirmed the link when he first played his new song to a subdued May Pang. Of the old Beatle hits, he remarked, 'Help!' was his favourite, and one day he would like to re-record it in the style of 'Scared'. After the gentle resolution of 'Bless You', jealousy is once more gnawing at his heart. He feels hatred, too, and casts a cold eye on himself, the man who will "sing out about love and peace" when his own emotions are a morass of negativity.

Brilliant and chilling it may be, but there is a certain theatricality about 'Scared', and only the sincerity of John's delivery prevents it tipping over into melodrama. A less assured, and therefore even bleaker, version of it can be found on *Menlove Avenue*. Of all the zany pseudonyms that John adopts in the credits to *Walls And Bridges* (Dwarf McDougal, Rev Fred Ghurkin, Dr Winston O'Reggae, etc), his namecheck on 'Scared' is the most apt — punning on the name of American crooner Mel Tormé, John becomes Mel Torment.

#9 DREAM

Speaking to the famous media theorist Marshall McLuhan in 1969, John offered an astute view of the artistic impulse. To write a song, he said, "is just like trying to describe a dream... Because we don't have telepathy, we try and describe the dream to each other, to verify to each other what we know, what we believe to be inside each other." In the classic '#9 Dream' he applied this approach quite literally. It's a mesmeric song that floats enchantingly in the space between peaceful sleep and fearful awakening.

'Yesterday' had come to Paul McCartney in a dream (or, at least, the melody did — he used the

John's first childhood home, 9 Newcastle Road in Liverpool. The number 9 came to acquire a mystic significance for him.

title 'Scrambled Eggs' until something better occurred to him) and some of John's song had a similar origin. He already had the basis of a melody, simply recycling his string arrangement for Harry Nilsson's version of 'Many Rivers To Cross' on *Pussy Cats*. (This song, by reggae star Jimmy Cliff, is itself a perfect expression of John's anguish at the time: "And this loneliness won't leave me alone.") He awoke one day and told May Pang that he'd dreamt about two women echoing his name, and also heard the strange refrain "Ah! böwakawa poussé, poussé." There was no translation for the words, but the female spirits were readily identifiable as May and Yoko.

When it came to recording the song, which was initially known as 'So Long', after John's opening line, May Pang was duly invited to whisper "John" at the relevant point. There is also a faintly murmured "Hare Krishna, George", by way of a greeting to John's old Beatle comrade, with whom he'd just had one of his periodic rows. It's likely, too, that Jesse Ed Davis's celestial guitar was a conscious tribute to Harrison's style. Once again, though, John was less than

John and May Pang attend the New York opening of the *Sgt Pepper* musical, 18 November 1974. She was his 'Sweet Bird of Paradox'.

generous to this music in 1980. In a BBC interview he referred to it as "craftsmanship writing" — which, in his terms, was not a compliment.

Why, though, was it finally called '#9 Dream'? Numerology, or the occult study of numbers and their hidden significance, was among the fringe interests that John had cultivated since the mid-Sixties. He fastened upon the number 9 as being especially important in his life. He was born on 9 October (as was his second son, Sean) and lived at 9 Newcastle Road in Liverpool. Among his earliest songwriting efforts was 'One after 909'. He named his most adventurous Beatle track 'Revolution 9'. Even the Dakota Building was on 72nd Street (seven plus two making nine). And he once predicted that he would die on the ninth day of the month. In the event, he was shot on 72nd Street and declared dead at 11.07 pm (the numerals again add up to nine) at the Roosevelt Hospital on Ninth Avenue. The date in New York, of course, was 8 December. But his native time zone is five hours ahead. In Liverpool, it was already morning — the morning of the ninth.

SURPRISE SURPRISE (SWEET BIRD OF PARADOX)

Amid so many messages to Yoko, it seems only right that May Pang should have one song explicitly devoted to her, the girl who gets John "through this God awful loneliness." May reports that John wrote this frankly sensual tribute to his "bird of paradise" at the outset of their affair in New York. She cried with emotion when he first played it to her. From the playful punning of its title to the "tweet-tweet, tweet-tweet" sounds at its fade (a jokey echo of the "beep beep" ending of the Beatles' 'Drive My Car') 'Surprise Surprise' brings a welcome upbeat to the album. In writing it, John had begun with yet another golden oldie on his mind — in this case it was the Diamonds' 1957 hit 'Little Darlin', though almost nothing of it survives in the finished article. Elton John attempted to add a backing vocal, but apparently found John's phrasing very difficult to match.

STEEL AND GLASS

The most avidly discussed number on *Walls And Bridges* was this cold-hearted masterpiece of invective. Soaked in those familiar, quasi-oriental strings, 'Steel and Glass' revisits the symphonic spite of *Imagine*'s anti-Paul epistle 'How Do You Sleep?'. So it's ironic, given his involvement in the prototype, that the presumed target of this equally nasty sequel should be Allen Klein.

John, however, was atypically coy about the victim's identity, and rather enjoyed the tease. Chuckling throatily over the song's mock-cowboy intro, he calls it a tale of "your friend and mine", while urgent whispers enquire, "Who is it? Who is it?". In a piece he wrote for Andy Warhol's *Interview* magazine, he taunts, "Next you'll be asking who 'Steel And Glass' is about. I can tell you who it isn't about, for instance, it's not about Jackie Kennedy, Mort Sahl, Sammy Davis, Bette Midler...Eartha Kitt, it's not about her either." Nor, he goes on to confirm, is it about Paul McCartney. Of his rift with Allen Klein, he merely says, "He was unfaithful."

For all their legendary fame, the Beatles did not earn huge amounts of money until Allen Klein took

Allen Klein rescued the Beatles' business affairs from chaos but Lennon turned upon him later in 'Steel and Glass'.

charge of their affairs. He was successful on their behalf to an extent that even Paul, who had been opposed to his appointment, had to acknowledge. But the manager's brash New York style was always out of place at Apple's HQ in Savile Row — where the last bastion of traditional English gentlemen met the new generation of Aquarian flower children. Klein, it goes without saying, was patently neither.

By 1974 he was back in Manhattan, where it is easier to picture him, at the desk of his top-floor office in the 41-storey "steel and glass" tower at 1700 Broadway. A year earlier he had fallen from favour with the other three Beatles, when his Apple contract lapsed. Soon, he and John were deep in litigation, issuing claim and counter-claim. The song paints the most unflattering portrait of an aggressive wheeler-dealer who is now losing his grip. An especially unfeeling touch is John's reference to the mother who "left you when you were small." Klein's own mother died of cancer when he was a baby.

In spite of it all, these two bruisers maintained a sneaking regard for one another. It's entirely possible that, despite their outward differences, they were kindred spirits. John actually stayed as Klein's house guest in 1974, even while litigation continued, and mere weeks before John wrote 'Steel And Glass'. The case was eventually settled in 1977.

According to photographer Bob Gruen, who had observed their peculiar friendship at close hand: "John told me that the contract for Allen to be their manager was one or two paragraphs on one sheet of paper. The contract to break up their original agreement was 87 pages... They liked Allen Klein before and they liked him after; it was just during the negotiations."

Lennon could be strangely unaware of how cruel he sometimes sounded. Perhaps he felt penitence later, when he described 'Steel And Glass' as "a son of 'How Do You Sleep?'" and denied that either song was directed at a single individual. He even claimed that 'Steel And Glass' was a dig at himself, just like his old song 'Nowhere Man'. But this was unconvincing. Lesser writers often have their songs mis-interpreted, but John used words with deadly precision. He might have regretted it afterwards, but his original meaning was usually unmistakable.

BEEF JERKY

Instrumental tracks are almost non-existent in Lennon's catalogue. It seems his love of music always came second to his passion for words. He could not see what performing was for, unless it was to say something. Nevertheless, a useful aspect of the "lost weekend" was John's new fondness for the fellowship of the recording studio. (Bear in mind that Yoko had been at his shoulder ever since

John on the roof of the New York apartment that he shared with May Pang, during Bob Gruen's photo session for the sleeve of *Walls and Bridges*.

the Beatles' "*White Album*" in 1968, which did little to improve the atmosphere at Abbey Road.) While 'Beef Jerky' is nothing special — just an efficiently funky, bustling rocker — it's a welcome interlude in *Walls And Bridges*, whose most tortured track was still to come. The relative jolliness of 'Beef Jerky' is underlined by John's sleeve credit, rearranging soul band Booker T & the MG's into his best gag so far, Booker Table & the Maitre D's.

NOBODY LOVES YOU (WHEN YOU'RE DOWN AND OUT)

This colossal ballad came out of a bad time in Lennon's life. Not only was he separated from the wife he loved, but his professional career was at its lowest ebb ever. A sprawling testament to John's cynicism and self-pity, 'Nobody Loves You (When You're Down And Out)' sounds nothing but sincere.

"That exactly expressed the whole period I was apart from Yoko," he told *Playboy*. He always imagined the number being sung by Frank Sinatra ("You need a song that isn't a piece of nothing") and its low-key, late night feel recalls the downbeat bar-fly of 'One For My Baby' or 'In The Wee Small Hours Of The Morning'. The title itself is a variant on Jimmie Cox's old blues standard 'Nobody Knows You When You're Down And Out' — John would be familiar with Eric Clapton's 1970 version on Derek & The Dominos' *Layla And Other Assorted Love Songs*.

As a grand statement of John's position in the mid-Seventies, 'Nobody Loves You' stands in a trilogy with 'God' (which opened the decade) and 'Starting Over' (which ended it). An ode to his marriage, it is also an address to his ageing generation, and the audience which has turned its back on him. In 'God' he had declared an end to the illusions of youth. In 'Starting Over' he would announce a renewed sense of purpose. But right now, in between those twin moments of resolution, he is simply exhausted, defeated by life's confusion.

Probably the song's key element is John's concept of himself as one who's "been across to the other side" and shared the experience. This, in other words, was the "shaman" role that he sensed himself fulfilling in a modern, media-driven world, where people's dreams are awakened and enacted by mass-entertainers. It was not a job he had ever particularly sought, and the demands of stardom had almost killed him. Ultimately, that is exactly what they did.

THE ROCK'N'ROLL ALBUM

The *Walls And Bridges* album actually ends with a snippet of the old Lee Dorsey song 'Ya Ya', with some tentative drumming by John's young son Julian, on a visit to New York with his mother Cynthia. The point of its inclusion was that it was owned by Morris Levy, but it failed to satisfy the publisher's demand that three of his numbers be covered.

Reluctantly, John now turned his attentions to the Spector tapes, despite their painful associations with his spell in LA. "These are awful,' he told May Pang. "I must have felt terrible when I did these." Nevertheless, with Levy at his heels, he agreed to revive the project and in late October he cleaned up what he could of the old sessions and recorded additional material to make a whole album. He later said of the exercise, "It was a contractual obligation to Morris Levy. It was a humiliation and I regret having to be in that position, but I did it." The Fifties idea had been so hot a year ago, especially after *American Graffiti*, and now it seemed only tedious.

But the vintage material came surprisingly easily to him. In his heart of hearts, John never forsook the

raw simplicity of Fifties music. In 1974, at the height of "pomp rock", he was foreshadowing the upsurge of punk. The Beatles' old producer George Martin was as surprised as anyone at Lennon's loyalty to rock's roots. He'd believed that after *Sgt Pepper* and *Abbey Road*, John would go on refining rock into "a mainstream of good new music. And I was disillusioned when that came to naught, because punk rock came along, the Sex Pistols and 'God Save The Queen' and everybody dropping their trousers. I thought, it's really not going this way after all. There was a rebellion against it. Even John Lennon didn't like the over-produced stuff. He wanted good old rousing rock'n'roll. So I was wrong, it didn't happen."

Yet John handles *Rock'N'Roll* with more nostalgia than outright passion. The rockers are low-voltage, like a work of mellow retrospection, and artfully airbrushed. With the exception of Lloyd Price's 'Just Because', which he'd not heard until Spector played it to him, the tracks selected paid tribute to John's teenage idols. Little Richard is heavily represented, with 'Rip It Up', 'Ready Teddy' and 'Slippin' And Slidin'; Chuck Berry is honoured with 'Sweet Little Sixteen' and the song that started all the trouble with Levy, 'You Can't Catch Me'. Larry Williams was a particular favourite — to the Beatles' covers of 'Dizzy Miss Lizzy', 'Slow Down' and 'Bad Boy', John now added 'Bony Moronie'. Other raves from the grave included Gene Vincent's 'Be-Bop-A-Lula' and Fats Domino's 'Ain't That A Shame'.

Of the final track listing only three cuts survived from Spector's troubled sessions. On sober reflection, Lennon said of his gifted, erratic collaborator: "I'm fond of his work a lot. His personality I'm not crazy

▲ **Lennon with producer Phil Spector during the mayhem of their doomed attempt to record a rock'n'roll oldies album.**

about." But Spector never lost a sense of his own legend. Speaking in 1976 he announced, "I only went into the studio to do one thing, and you can tell this to John Lennon. *They* were making records, but I was making Art..."

The *Rock'N'Roll* cover carried a beautiful archive photograph of John as a young teddy boy, standing in a Hamburg doorway. Looking at the picture in 1974, he felt his life had come full cycle. "I thought, is this some kind of karmic thing? Here I am with this old picture of me in Hamburg from '61, and I'm ending as I started, singing this straight rock'n'roll stuff."

Jürgen Vollmer's classic 1961 shot of John in a Hamburg doorway, later used for the cover of *Rock'n'Roll*.

DOUBLE FANTASY

7

ALBUM

DOUBLE FANTASY
'(Just Like) Starting Over'
'Cleanup Time'
'I'm Losing You'
'Beautiful Boy (Darling Boy)'
'Watching The Wheels'
'Woman'
'Dear Yoko'

The 1975 Grammy night was John and Yoko's first joint outing since their reunion. They lined up with David Bowie, Art Garfunkel, Paul Simon and Roberta Flack.

"Our separation was a failure." With that typically Lennonesque verdict, John put the public seal on his reunion with Yoko. Consummating the process which began after Elton John's Madison Square show, John moved back into his Dakota home in early 1975. He continued to visit his mistress May Pang, sporadically at least, for some time afterwards. But, from now until the end of his days, he was officially reinstated in the "Johnandyoko" partnership.

In March 1975, recollecting the mayhem he had only narrowly survived, John told *Rolling Stone*, "This last year has been extraordinary for me... I feel like I've been on Sinbad's voyage and I've battled all those monsters and I've got back." With no little symbolism, 1975 began with the formal dissolution, in London's High Court, of the Beatles as a legal entity. And, within a month, Yoko became pregnant. The couple's only child, Sean, was conceived within days of John's return to the marital fold.

Domesticity beckoned at last. But there was still work to be done before he could relax. In February his old adversary Morris Levy released an album of John's *Rock'N'Roll* sessions, entitled *Roots*. Lennon and his record company, EMI/Capitol, promptly sued Levy for his unauthorised release and issued the official version on 17 February. John and Yoko made their first public appearance together on 1 March, attending the Grammy Awards ceremony where they were pictured in the skeletal company of David Bowie, the rising superstar of the moment.

Just a few weeks previously, John had helped Bowie complete his *Young Americans* album in New York, playing guitar on a version of his own 'Across The Universe' and a new song that the pair co-wrote with Bowie's guitarist Carlos Alomar. Improvised around a scratchy funk riff, 'Fame' was a bleak meditation on the barren nature of celebrity, made as John was walking away from stardom and Bowie was rushing to embrace it. The one disillusioned, the other ambitious, they were scarcely singing from the same hymn sheet, but the match of old master and young pretender was effective. John's touch proved Midas-like, granting Bowie a Number 1 hit and making the singer's name in America.

On 13 June Lennon played before an audience for the final time in his life. On a TV tribute to the entertainment mogul Lew Grade, introduced by the comedian Dave Allen, John led a band in sci-fi costumes through perfunctory renditions of 'Imagine' and, from the *Rock'N'Roll* album, 'Slippin and Slidin' and Ben E. King's 'Stand By Me'. The invited audience, dressed to the nines, sat at their tables and applauded politely. It was all a million miles from the Cavern or Hamburg's Star Club, and a strangely anti-climactic end to John's career as a live performer.

Great news came on 7 October when the New York Supreme Court overturned John's deportation order and asked the Immigration Service to reconsider their case. "Lennon's four-year battle to remain in our country is a testament to his faith in that American Dream," they noted. Even more momentous was John's 35th birthday, 9 October, which also saw the birth of Sean Taro Ono Lennon. Facing the reporters John said, "I feel higher than the Empire State Building."

With the simultaneous breakthrough in his immigration fight, the stage was set for John's withdrawal from the wider world. On 24 October, as if to emphasise that another chapter was ended, he issued the *Shaved Fish* compilation of his post-Beatle hits. Like the other three Beatles, he'd been haunted by the likelihood that his entire life after 30 would be a mere appendix to the Big Book. By now, though, he could face that prospect calmly. He allowed whole weeks to pass in which he did no more than play with the baby, and potter about the apartment. He had become a "househusband".

In July 1976 he was granted US resident's status — "It's great to be legal again," he quipped, clutching the precious Green Card — and was promised full citizenship by 1981. Having acquired a mantle of respectability, in 1977 he attended the inauguration gala of President Jimmy Carter — a sign of how much the establishment and the old troublemaker had come together. In '79, the former scourge of authority donated $1,000 to buy bullet-proof vests for the New York police. While Yoko assumed the role of John's business representative, investing the family fortune in real estate and farm animals, John used his new freedom to make several trips to foreign countries, though never to Britain. In 1979 the

Taping the TV special, *Salute To Lew Grade*, on 13 June 1975 — the last time John performed before an audience.

John at home in the Dakota Building, his New York refuge in the final years of his life.

other three Beatles played together at Eric Clapton's wedding party in England; John claimed that he would have attended but did not find out in time.

It was Yoko who encouraged John to travel, hoping to bolster her man's fragile sense of independence. His routes were seemingly dictated by her readings of the Tarot cards and ancient Japanese beliefs concerning the magical validity of directions. But his 1980 journey to Bermuda was the most important, being the prelude to his long-awaited comeback. During his stay on the island he wrote or refined most of the songs he would record later that year. Strolling in June through the Botanical Gardens he came across a flower, the "Double Fantasy" freesia whose name encapsulated the idea behind the couple's next project. It would be a jointly-credited album in the form of a "Heart Play", or a dialogue between John's songs and Yoko's.

In an August press release the couple announced that *Double Fantasy* would be an "exploration of sexual fantasies between men and women". It would be a concept album of sorts, and John joked that they could have called themselves "Ziggy" and "Tommy", after the famous rock fictions of Bowie and The Who, but they wanted something true to their actual lives. And the underlying reason for his return to music? That was simple, he said: "You breathe in, you breathe out."

First he would need a new record company. Every label was interested in John Lennon, but the serious

John, May Pang and Sean at Palm Beach.

contenders were dismayed to learn he planned a joint effort with Yoko. One man with faith, however, was the young executive David Geffen. A high-flyer who retired prematurely when diagnosed as having cancer, he'd returned in 1980 with a clean bill of health and his very own Geffen label. Among his first signings was Elton John (later clients would include Guns N'Roses and Nirvana) and, on 22 September, John and Yoko duly came aboard.

Sessions began on 4 August at New York's Hit Factory, supervised by John's old engineer Jack Douglas. Despite approaches from other former colleagues, Jesse Ed Davis and Elephant's Memory included, Lennon chose a new team featuring guitarists Hugh McCracken and Bowie sideman Earl Slick. With a sleeve dedication to everyone who'd helped them stay in the USA, John and Yoko's *Double Fantasy* appeared on 17 November, to a generally lukewarm response from the critics. Still, the initial sales were fair and would, of course, receive a gruesome boost in the weeks to follow.

John was reinvigorated by his comeback. He now gave a series of lengthy, entertaining interviews, and soon turned his attentions towards producing a new Yoko track, 'Walking On Thin Ice'. Yoko herself would later recall: "John and I were gloriously happy in the first week of December. *Double Fantasy* was in the Top 10. It was just a matter of time for it to go up to Number 1, since we still had two weeks to Christmas and it was selling well. We kept saying,

Roy Orbison, whose ballad 'Only the Lonely' was affectionately parodied by Lennon in '(Just Like) Starting Over'.

'We did it, we did it,' and hugged each other."

In conversation he hinted at a world tour in 1981. He'd see Britain, too, but there was no need to rush. "What do you think," he teased one interviewer, "that it's going to vanish?". He confessed, too, that he didn't understand the new decimal currency. On 7 December he was seen to grow emotional as he leafed through a book about Liverpool. On 8 December he and Yoko went to the studio to work on 'Thin Ice'. Meanwhile, in all the renewed activity, growing numbers of fans were braving the New York winter. Clutching album covers and autograph books, they gathered around the doors of the Dakota.

(JUST LIKE) STARTING OVER

Back in 1970 John Lennon's first solo album began with a tolling bell. Now, in a deliberate echo, he opened the final album of his life with another bell. This time it was no slowed-down harbinger of doom, but the benevolent tinkling of a traditional Japanese "wishing bell" and the track it introduced, '(Just Like) Starting Over', was in every sense a message of renewal. If the mournful 1970 album proclaimed the purging of his past, John's new song faced the future with a heart full of hope.

Building on a 1979 Dakota demo called 'My Life', John developed the track during his 1980 summer holiday in Bermuda, while Sean played in the sun and Yoko looked after business back in New York. His central theme is of a long-standing couple whose love is strong, but who need time out to recapture the spirit of their early romance. John mentioned in a BBC interview that he took the title from a country song. This would presumably have been 'Starting Over Again' — actually written by the disco star Donna Summer — which became a Number 1 country hit for Dolly Parton in late May of 1980, at the time John was assembling songs for his album. Ironically, though, Dolly's ballad tells the story of a middle-aged couple who cap their 30 years of marriage by deciding to divorce.

At one point, John considered ditching the line "It's time to spread our wings" in case people assumed a reference to Paul McCartney's band of the Seventies. In reality the career that is charted by '(Just Like) Starting Over' is John's. Its spacious echoes and thudding drums were a subliminal reminder of the old solo Lennon of 'Instant Karma!' And, since he was making a fresh start, why not go even further back, to the pre-Beatles music he had loved in his youth? Dubbing himself "Elvis Orbison", he camped up his recording with old-fashioned touches, lovingly borrowed from Roy Orbison's 'Only The Lonely' and Elvis Presley's 'I Want You, I Need You, I Love You'.

Thus the "tough, unsentimental" Beatle once more revealed his weakness for nostalgia. He would stress that '(Just Like) Starting Over' was addressed to his own generation. "All we are saying," he told *Playboy*, "is this is what's happening to us." Yoko elaborated, explaining that the Sixties gave people a taste for freedom, but the Seventies had seen men and women in conflict, destroying their relationships and damaging family life. In the Eighties, she and John were voicing the hope that people would begin to find one another again.

In the event, these were ideas that Lennon never had the chance to investigate more deeply. Though it hints at what might have become important strands in his thinking — the value of family, the need for social cohesion, the role of responsibilities as distinct from rights — the song's delivery was perhaps too whimsical to stake any claim to greatness. At the time of its release, on 27 October 1980, much of its appeal was simply the delight of hearing his voice once more.

CLEANUP TIME

On the phone from Bermuda to his producer Jack Douglas in New York, John discussed a seeming trend for people to give up the drink and drug excesses of the Seventies. Said Douglas: "Well, it's cleanup time, right?" Taken by the phrase, John replied, "It sure is." With that he ended the conversation, went straight to his piano and "just started boogieing." Now that he had a tune and a title he needed a story. Turning his thoughts to home, he hit upon a description of the Lennons' life at the Dakota, in their "Palace of Versailles", like the king and queen of the old nursery rhyme 'Sing A Song Of Sixpence'. ("The King was in the counting house, counting out his money/The Queen was in the parlour, eating bread and honey".)

This was a scenario he had visited before, in the Beatles' 'Cry Baby Cry'. But here was a twist in the tale. Yoko and John had undergone a role reversal in their marriage — man and wife had become businesswoman and househusband. She was in the counting house, seeing to their finances, while John was in the kitchen making bread of the other sort... Or so they liked to say. It's known that Yoko did become a formidable negotiator, but there is less hard evidence that John turned into the apron-wearing homemaker and childminder that he liked to pretend. In truth, Yoko had never been terribly domestic and John was incapable of concentrating on business.

A question mark remains, however, over whose 'Cleanup Time' it actually was. By John's account he was making a general observation. But the song is clearly set at home. The Lennons always professed to have been free of drugs from the year of Sean's birth, 1975. Even so, a 1988 *Rolling Stone* article that helped to demolish some of Albert Goldman's wilder theories about the couple, could be interpreted as an admission by Yoko of a brief relapse in late 1979. "It was not a good thing to do," she conceded. "But at the same time, I'm proud that I conquered it."

I'M LOSING YOU

This was a number that John first tried in 1978, as 'Stranger's Room'. As such, it has the air of some adulterous escapade. But John preferred to claim his song had its beginnings in Bermuda, after he'd tried to phone Yoko in New York. Yoko visited John only briefly during the trip, returning to her office at the Dakota, where John found it frustratingly difficult to contact her. Failing to connect, he said later, "I was just mad as hell, feeling lost and separate." He likened it to his state of isolation in the mid-Seventies "lost weekend", or even to the loss of his mother.

Still, 'I'm Losing You' is primarily a song about the experience of domestic conflict. The Lennons were often accused of using *Double Fantasy* and its attendant interviews to paint a falsely benign portrait of their marriage. But, as ever, their songs make no attempt to varnish the truth. Whenever John and Yoko attained harmony they always celebrated the fact, but if they failed occasionally, their failure was never disguised. The unflinching realism of 'I'm Losing You' is firmly reinforced by the angry song it segues into, Yoko's sneering goodbye 'I'm Moving On'. Linked by a harsh sequence of electronic bleeps and sharing Earl Slick's jagged, nagging guitar lick, the two tracks represent a full-on confrontation. It's an instance where the "Heart Play" dialogue idea works well.

Small wonder that 'I'm Losing You' took John back to his dark night of the soul in 1973 — the year that Yoko wrote 'I'm Moving On' and promptly kicked him out. We cannot know if history was about to repeat itself, but 'I'm Losing You' is proof, at least, that *Double Fantasy* is a work of greater emotional complexity than many of its critics have been prepared to admit.

BEAUTIFUL BOY (DARLING BOY)

For John the central event of 1975 had been his wife's pregnancy. It came, of course, after years of miscarriages, and in spite of John's belief that his own system was too weakened ever to sire a child again. His first son, Julian, had been unplanned — a fact he tactlessly referred to by remarking, "Ninety percent of the people on this planet were born out of a bottle of whisky on a Saturday night." But Sean was the child that he and Yoko had longed for, and they lavished care upon her pregnancy. Guided by the same Chinese doctor who John claimed had weaned him off drugs, they put their faith in clean living, macrobiotic diets and acupuncture.

In Sean they saw the word made flesh. Their union, the union of East and West, had been made incarnate in a way that, previously, they could only sing about. After the baby's birth, John's artistic output slackened considerably, but he welcomed the paternal responsibilities he'd never borne for Julian. A genuinely touching lullaby, gracefully embellished by some Caribbean steel drumming, 'Beautiful Boy's words and music came to John more or less simultaneously, a sign of its easy sincerity. He took pride in the time they spent together during the first five years of Sean's life. He believed the next generation would be happier if more parents could do likewise. But he resented Mick Jagger for suggesting that John had sacrificed his music to stay at home, as if it were not possible to do both.

Among the pearls of wisdom that John passes on to his son is the famous line, "Life is what happens to you while you're busy making other plans." According to the British astrologer Patric Walker, this was a precept of the Islamic creed Sufi, that he shared with John "over coffee in New York one morning". John first used it in a 1979 song, 'My Life', which he later abandoned. In the light of impending events, it's a line that still leaps out with unwelcome force.

As to Julian, John felt guilt about his lack of active parenting: "It's not the best relationship between father and son, but it is there... I hadn't seen Julian

John with his 'Beautiful Boy', Sean. He advised his son: "Life is what happens to you while you're busy making other plans."

grow up at all, and now there's a 17-year-old on the phone about motorbikes." Julian Lennon later commented, "The last year, I would say, was the best. I was growing older, I began to understand things a lot more and understand Dad too... Towards the end we were definitely getting closer."

In 1995, Paul McCartney recalled a Beatle holiday with John and Julian in Greece. Paul was playing happily with the boy, which made John curious: "He took me aside and said, 'How do you do that?'. Well, luckily towards the end of his life, John had found out how to do that."

Lennon in March 1975, at the outset of his five-year period, "just watching the wheels".

WATCHING THE WHEELS

In 1972, three years before his own disappearance from public life, Lennon had defended Bob Dylan from those who criticised the singer for opting out of his role as spokesman for the counter culture: "Dylan exists with or without the Movement. We owe him a great deal of things... It does not matter that Dylan has done nothing for six months or that he chooses to rest for a year, or that he is going through a psychological crisis, or that he has had an accident, or that he wants to live with his children and his family. Dylan has done what he has done and he continues. We ought to let him have a little time to breathe."

The words were remarkably prophetic of John's position in the five-year hiatus leading up to the release of *Double Fantasy*. Yet his almost total absence from the scene was really without parallel in a rock star of such magnitude. When Elvis Presley joined the US Army for two years from 1958, his career was kept on the boil with photo-calls, a Hollywood movie, re-issues and even new records cut while he was on leave. Bob Dylan was only a true recluse for 18 months, following a motorbike accident in 1966. In the late Seventies Bruce Springsteen, John's nearest rival as rock standard bearer, had a lengthy lay-off in between *Born To Run* and *Darkness On The Edge Of Town*, but continued touring in the interim.

Meanwhile Lennon's profile was authentically low. And despite his previous words of encouragement, he was privately scornful of "company men" like Dylan, Jagger and McCartney who all contrived to keep the product coming. When his EMI deal expired in January 1976, he was out of contract for the first time since the Beatles signed up 14 years earlier. He

In the late Seventies, Lennon watched the rise of Bruce Springsteen, which coincided with his own retirement. He later wished that he'd made *Double Fantasy* more rocky, like Springsteen's records.

was the only member of the group not to carry on: Paul renewed his deal, George went to A&M and Ringo signed with Polydor and Atlantic.

In 'Watching The Wheels', John explained how content he had been "just sitting here... watching shadows on the wall" while the outside world deplored his apparent lethargy. We know that he was not the Howard Hughes character of legend — he travelled extensively and enjoyed a fairly active social life. Nor was it true that he abandoned music completely, in spite of his subsequent suggestions to the contrary — in fact he wrote numerous songs and made many demo recordings. But he used the five-year holiday to balance out the excessive publicity of his earlier life, to take stock of his experiences, and to recover from an existence as turbulent as anyone had ever known.

Media pleadings and the consternation of his fans had little effect. Doubtless he was aware of the *New Musical Express* cover story of 14 January 1978 which demanded, "Where the hell are you, John Lennon?". His absence was felt especially keenly in Britain: "John, plenty of us here have found your reluctance to use your green card to at least pay us a courtesy call less than excusable." The journalist, Neil Spencer, went on to note how much the UK's punk revolution owed

John and Yoko in November 1980, taking their last walk in Central Park together, on the site that was later re-named Strawberry Fields in his honour.

to Lennon's influence: "They started the revolution without you, mate. But then you started it without waiting for anyone else. It took the rest of us a long time to catch up — but that's no reason to opt out now."

Even his peers among the rock aristocracy were bemused by John's inactivity. "I couldn't believe it," he said. "They were acting like mothers-in-law." He told *Newsweek* that the comments he read reminded him of his teachers' reports. On one of his several visits to Japan, Lennon held a press conference to explain his inactivity. "We've basically decided, without a great decision, to be with our baby as much as we can until we feel we can take the time off to indulge ourselves creating things outside the family. Maybe when he's three, four or five then we'll think about creating something else other than the child."

On 27 May 1979, the Lennons placed a full-page ad in papers in London, New York and Tokyo. Entitled "A love letter from John and Yoko," it was addressed "to people who ask us what, when and why." In its text the couple described "the Spring Cleaning of our minds! It was a lot of work" and once more aired their old belief in the power of wishes. Their conclusion: "We are all part of the sky, more so than of the ground. Remember, we love you." Having begun in demo form (as 'I'm Crazy') that same year, 'Watching The Wheels' was John's musical version of the "love letter" that he had placed in the newspapers.

A hankering for the quiet life was not new to John's thinking. He'd often spoken wistfully of a peaceful retirement with Yoko, perhaps in a cottage in Ireland. As early as 1969, at the height of his media-saturated peace campaigning, John told his interviewer Miles of a TV documentary he'd just watched, about a man training a falcon at some remote retreat in Cornwall: "And I thought, God almighty, it's all I want, really... I always have this dream of being the artist in a little cottage and I didn't do any of this publicity or anything; my real thing is just write a little poetry and do a few oils. It just seemed like such a dream, living in a cottage and wandering in the trees."

WOMAN

On its simplest level 'Woman' was another in Lennon's series of apologies to Yoko for the most oafish excesses of his past. But he was keen that people read the song as being dedicated to womankind in general. The track opens with an adaptation of Mao Tse-Tung's adage that women and men are complementary halves of the sky — or, as John put it, "without each other, there's nothing." At the *Double Fantasy* sessions John explained 'Woman' to his musicians as being "early Motown/Beatles '64. It's for your mother or your sister, anyone of the female race. That's who you're singing to."

Among the most enduring and most accessible recordings of his last year, John always thought of 'Woman' as the album's "Beatle track". He described it as an Eighties update of his 1965 *Rubber Soul* song 'Girl', the only Beatle song that Cynthia Lennon believed that he had written specifically about her. Although he'd expressed pro-feminist feelings in earlier songs, John said he had only recently "put my body where my mouth was" by acting out his beliefs. 'Woman Is The Nigger Of The World', he confessed, was no more than an intellectual position. Not until the late Seventies had he made much effort to put the theory into practice. Of the books which influenced him, John acknowledged *The First Sex* by Elizabeth Gould Davis.

There were many examples of Lennon's jealous cruelty, and even outright violence, in his dealings with Yoko, May Pang, and Cynthia, as well as with the innumerable girls and women who had crossed his path in the last 40 years. He was a man, he considered, who had been waited on by women all his life, and had often responded with abominable ingratitude. "My history of relationships with women is a very poor one," he told *Playboy*. "Very macho, very typical of a certain type of man, I suppose, which is very sensitive and insecure but acting aggressive and macho. You know, trying to cover up the feminine side, which I still have a tendency to do... I tend to put on my cowboy boots when I'm insecure, whereas now I'm in sneakers and it's comfy."

In the same interview, he angrily refuted the notion that Yoko rather dominated him: "Rubbish... The only one who controls me is me, and that's just barely possible." But he said of feminism, "the real changes are coming. I am the one who has come a long way. I was the pig. And it is a relief not to be a pig." As to his recent "househusband" phase, it was "the wave of the future, and I'm glad to be in on the forefront of that too."

DEAR YOKO

Kicking off with a playful Buddy Holly gurgle, 'Dear Yoko' closes John's contribution to *Double Fantasy* (the album's last words went to Yoko, in 'Every Man Has a Woman Who Loves Him' and 'Hard Times Are Over'). It shares the same spirit of throwaway gaiety as 'Oh Yoko!', which had concluded *Imagine* nine years beforehand. This song was written while John was in Bermuda, "miles at sea" and missing his absent wife. So it may have another parallel with 'Oh Yoko!', which was originally conceived in a bout of

John at one of his last public engagements, a dinner in New York City, November 1980.

insecurity. As 'I'm Losing You' had shown, there were moments in Lennon's tropical sojourn when he feared desertion, and 'Dear Yoko' sounds like another instance of John singing to keep his spirits up.

It must be said that 'Dear Yoko' does not match its predecessor's infectious gusto, but John declared himself well satisfied. "It says it all," he told *Playboy*. "The track's a nice track and it happens to be about my wife, instead of 'Dear Sandra' or some other person that another singer would sing about who may or may not exist." In other words, whatever its musical merits, the song has the virtue of having sprung out of real life. And for John Lennon, that was what mattered. Everything else was mere "craftsmanship".

For all we know, he might have come to disown the song. He never looked back at his music as anything more than "work in progress". He'd even dreamed of re-recording 'Strawberry Fields Forever'. But he never got the opportunity. On 8 December 1980, a half-crazy character named Mark Chapman stood with those die-hard fans outside the Dakota, harbouring thoughts of Lennon's "dishonesty". At 10.49 that evening the Lennons' automobile pulled up at Number 1, West 72nd Street, and Chapman committed the act that would, however temporarily, make him as famous as the man he had once worshipped.

18

MILK AND HONEY

ALBUM

MILK AND HONEY
'I'm Stepping Out'
'I Don't Wanna Face It'
'Nobody Told Me'
'Borrowed Time'
'(Forgive Me) My Little Flower Princess'
'Grow Old With Me'

JOHN LENNON'S LEGACY
Tribute records, posthumous compilations, rarities, the 1994/1995 Beatle sessions

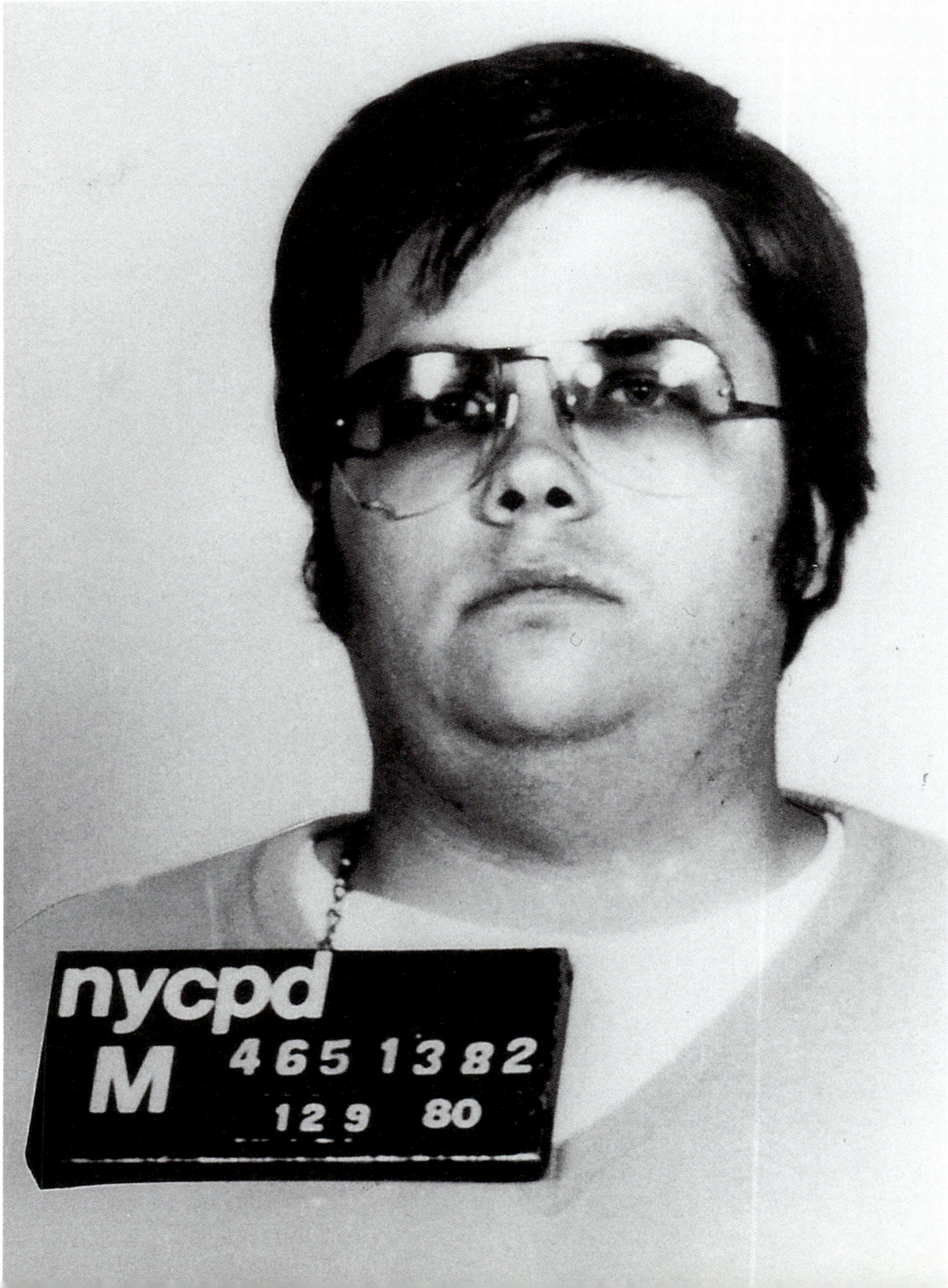

Lennon's assassin, Mark Chapman, the morning after he fired the fatal shots outside the Dakota Building.

"Do you mean that he is sleeping?" said Yoko Ono to the medical staff at Roosevelt Hospital. Her husband had been shot, with five bullets to the chest, as he was entering the Dakota less than half an hour before. Now, in her bewilderment, she could not believe that he was dead. The time was around 11.15pm, 8 December 1980, and John Lennon's murderer, Mark Chapman, was already under arrest, having submitted himself to the police without a struggle.

In the days that followed John's assassination, Yoko's grief and disbelief were shared in some measure by many millions of people. Lennon's place in the collective imagination went deeper than mere celebrity, however grand the scale. His sudden loss brought a sense of bereavement with an almost spiritual dimension. He had embodied the soul of his times, and most who shared those times discovered that they loved him more than they knew.

On other levels life went on. A mortuary assistant took a sneak photograph of John on the slab, selling it to newspapers for $10,000. Still, as Yoko noted, John at least looked peaceful in the picture, which was strangely reminiscent of the profile portrait on *Imagine*. Media tributes proliferated, while the newstands clogged with hastily written souvenirs — the majority displaying a peculiar blend of sincerity and opportunism. On 14 December there were

Mourning fans at a silent vigil in Central Park, 14 December. On the same day a simultaneous ceremony was held in Liverpool.

"Stepping out" in 1977, this time to the first night of a New York dance week. Lennon's later years were not as reclusive as he sometimes suggested.

simultaneous vigils in Lennon's two hometowns, Liverpool and New York, attended by thousands of mourners. Within a year, Mark Chapman would be sentenced to 20 years to life.

By the standards of the music industry, the treatment of John Lennon's catalogue has been tasteful. The market was not bombarded with shoddy compilations, and his unfinished tracks have appeared only slowly — in the case of 'Free As A Bird', it took 15 years. "Tribute" records are another tradition in pop music, and normally range from the cynical to the mawkish. Lennon raised the whole standard of pop, so it's fitting he inspired some tribute records of the highest order.

First, though, there are the tracks that he began recording in the *Double Fantasy* sessions, presumably intending to finish them afterwards. In January 1984, Yoko released six of John's songs on *Milk And Honey*. Alternating with new tracks of her own, they were sub-titled "A Heart Play", in the dialogue tradition of *Double Fantasy* itself. Although they're unrefined recordings, being only works in progress, they are complete John Lennon songs. And, as ever, they diarise his hopes and fears with compelling honesty.

I'M STEPPING OUT

As with all *Milk And Honey's* tracks, 'I'm Stepping Out' is credited to John and Yoko as co-writers, but the rough good humour sounds more Lennon than Ono. Clearly its theme of joyous escape was close to his heart: it was the very first number attempted at the *Double Fantasy* sessions. The official Lennon comeback is simply bursting with the pent-up energies of five years spent away from a recording studio. It also reminds us he was not the total "homebody" of cherished myth.

Practically gabbling with excitement, John sets out his stall at the very beginning. This is the story of a "househusband" who's gone stir crazy at home, looking after kids and cats and watching summer repeats on the TV. For the sake of his own sanity he's going to beat his cabin fever, dress up tonight and paint the town red. Oh, and don't worry, he'll "be in before 1 ... or 2 ... or 3."

Such a merry manifesto of independence is a happy contrast to his many songs of meek contrition, and suggests that he was never really the Hermit of West 72nd Street. Parts of the song date back to 1977, eventually reaching the demo stage in Bermuda. Even by the end it was a fairly knockabout recording which he might have improved upon later on, but it skips along in high spirits and it's packed with persuasive little details. Thus he decides he'll kick over the traces and leave a rude message on his answering machine. Then, with baby and cats pacified, he'll treat himself to a longed-for cigarette. A devout smoker, Lennon trusted that his macrobiotic regime would protect him against cancer. "Of course," he added, casually, "if we die, we're wrong."

I DON'T WANNA FACE IT

Another Bermuda demo with its roots in 1977, 'I Don't Wanna Face It' was never quite perfected at the Hit Factory sessions. But again it's a telling insight into Lennon's Dakota years. Plenty of people criticised John Lennon, but he usually got there first, and did it better. The litany of put downs is, in this case, clearly self-directed. He is the man who looks in the mirror and sees nobody there. Like the classically self-righteous radical, he proclaims his love of humanity but just can't stand people. And he sings for a supper that he doesn't know how to make. Here is John, still "with one eye on the Hall of Fame", coming to realise that his ambitions no longer lie in that arena. At any rate, not for now.

"John had periods when he renounced the whole thing," says Paul McCartney, who was in touch with Lennon during the late Seventies. As with any new kick he'd discovered, John was passionately evangelical: "I remember him phoning me and saying, 'Look lad, it's the most difficult thing to renounce our fame.

We're so hooked on fame, but it's great, you should kick it over.' And I'm going, 'Hmm, do tell me, what do you mean here?'. I listened to him but after about a year of that he was back. And what was his famous line? 'This housewife wants a job.'"

NOBODY TOLD ME

When Lennon first sketched this song it was called 'Everybody's Talkin', Nobody's Talkin', perhaps inspired by the title of Harry Nilsson's hit. The verse words present a string of paradoxes ("There's always something happenin'/ And nothing goin' on.") until, at the chorus, John throws up his hands in exasperation. 'Nobody Told Me' is fine, sturdy rock'n'roll, and proof that his cynical wit was not extinct.

With its catalogue of daily frustrations, 'Nobody Told Me' is another signal that John's last years were not so blissfully mellow as he suggested. (Another demo from the same era, called 'You Save My Soul', actually implies he was nearly driven to suicide.) During his career, Lennon learned to his cost that it's foolish to be totally open with the media. His "bigger than Jesus" quote brought endless trouble; talking about drugs invited more problems with the authorities; references to his family would often cause them pain. By 1980 John was adept at setting his interviewers' agenda, painting the picture which he and Yoko had agreed upon. But the songs he wrote seemed immune to this self-censorship. Their candour is like something he cannot help.

There's some evidence that John intended to give 'Nobody Told Me' to Ringo. If that's true, it would have been one of Lennon's better presents to his old drummer, who'd been the recipient of less-than-classic compositions. As recently as 1976 John had donated the lacklustre 'Cookin' (in the Kitchen of Love)' to Ringo's *Rotogravure* album. In 1974 he contributed the title track to *Goodnight Vienna*. And, a year before that, he offered Ringo 'I'm the Greatest' — a song he'd originally written for himself, before deciding that Mohammed Ali's famous line might sound less arrogant coming from Ringo Starr than from John Lennon.

Possibly the oddest line in 'Nobody Told Me' concerns "the little yellow idol". In fact it's a near-quote from a 1911 poem, The Green Eye Of The Yellow God ("There's a one-eyed yellow idol to the north of Katmandu") written by J. Milton Hayes, who died in the year of Lennon's birth. Like Kipling's work, this poem was familiar to people of John's parents' generation, a staple of pub and parlour recitations in John's formative years.

BORROWED TIME

While the island of Bermuda is not actually in the Caribbean, the old British colony had a sufficiently West Indian feel to put John in the mood for reggae. He whiled away the 1980 summer trip listening to Bob Marley, the superstar of Jamaican music whose iconic status and crusading role made him, in effect, John Lennon's black counterpart. The two men never met — in fact Marley was to die just six months after John — but their paths would surely have converged in the Eighties — had they not both met such premature ends. John was always fond of Marley's *Burnin'*, the 1972 album which brought the Wailers to global notice, especially when John's friend Eric Clapton covered 'I Shot The Sheriff'. It was another *Burnin'* track, 'Hallelujah Time' which gave John the idea for 'Borrowed Time'.

Bearing in mind that his song never got beyond the band rehearsal stage, we can forgive the cod-tropical accent John attempts. 'Borrowed Time' is an evocative piece of writing; it's a pity we'll never hear it in definitive form. That said, it's less like reggae than generic West Indian easy listening. Lennon spent the last years trying to widen his horizons. He enjoyed Muzak, because there were no words to distract him; he explored Japanese folk music and Indian music. He defended disco from detractors who thought it too simplistic and repetitive — those were the very

▲ **Bob Marley, who died within six months of John, was an equally inspirational figure, and one source of Lennon's 'Borrowed Time'.**

qualities that had turned him on to Little Richard.

Reggae was a style he'd championed since the Sixties. In its earlier forms — ska, bluebeat and rock-steady — the music thrived in British clubs, imported by Caribbean immigrants, then taken up by London tastemakers such as the Beatles. The group made a few facetious stabs at it, including 'Ob-La-Di, Ob-La-Da' and the *Anthology II* take of 'You Know My Name (Look Up The Number)'. But John was frustrated in his efforts to make convincing reggae on his solo albums, finding his US musicians unused to it and the US audience unready for it. Nor was he the only white rocker to find that loving reggae was not the same as mastering it.

It's the optimism and contentment of 'Borrowed Time' which make it so endearing. With a poignancy we need not labour, John reflects on life's brevity. He's outgrown the confusion of youth, and believes it's "good to be older". The wisdom of age has shown him how little he really knows, but he's free, at least, of illusions and distractions: "The future is brighter and now is the hour." John's life was cruelly abbreviated but it's satisfying that his body of work should contain this song. Complementing the frank unhappiness of earlier works, it introduces a final note of wholeness and fulfillment.

Lennon had only contempt for the supposed glamour of early death. He was scornful of Neil Young's 1979 *Rust Never Sleeps* song 'My My Hey Hey' which extolled the Sex Pistols' Johnny Rotten and the notion that it's better to burn out than to fade away. Referring to the recent death of Rotten's sidekick, Lennon demanded, "Sid Vicious died for what? So that we might rock? It's garbage."

(FORGIVE ME) MY LITTLE FLOWER PRINCESS

It's understandable that Yoko should be partial to John's most abject songs of submission, but there is a case for saying that '(Forgive Me) My Little Flower Princess' ought to have been left in peace. John recorded this tale early in the *Double Fantasy* sessions and did not return to it. Even had he done so, it's difficult to see how it might be salvaged.

One of Lennon's more unlikely influences, the Victorian poet Robert Browning, author of the line "Grow old along with me."

GROW OLD WITH ME

John's 'Grow Old With Me' is preceded by a companion Yoko song, 'Let Me Count The Ways', Her title quotes Elizabeth Barrett Browning's *Sonnets From The Portuguese*: "How do I love thee?/Let me count the ways..." John responds with a song derived from another poem, *Rabbi Ben Ezra*, by Elizabeth's husband Robert Browning: "Grow old along with me! The best is yet to be." The Ono-Lennons apparently identified with the Brownings, a devoted couple who wrote some of the most admired poetry in 19th-century English literature. Yoko's next track, the album's finale 'You're the One', offers a few more analogies: to the mocking world, she and John were Laurel & Hardy; in their own imaginations they were the storm-tossed lovers of *Wuthering Heights*, Cathy and Heathcliff.

With its chorus of "God bless our love", and John's simple piano part, 'Grow Old with Me' has the Sunday school air of a Victorian hymn. The sad irony of its central image ("man and wife together, world without end") echoes its inspiration: Browning's poem first appeared in 1864, three years after his wife's death. John once told his interviewer Barry Miles of his dreams for the future. "I really can't wait to be old," he said. "You do your best and then there is a time when you do slow down and it seems nice. I always look forward to being an old couple of about 60, just remembering everything. I suppose we'll still be cursing because we're in a wheelchair."

JOHN LENNON'S LEGACY

Lennon approved of punk music, but was unexcited by it. He thought he'd sung it himself at the Cavern and in Hamburg. Perhaps he should have investigated the New York acts who were making real innovations in the late Seventies — Television, Talking Heads, Blondie, the Ramones, Patti Smith. From his Dakota window he could see across to the Bronx, where rap was being born. He would probably have loved it as much as reggae. Just before he died, he made an effort to update his tastes by checking out the Manhattan dance clubs. Some of that contemporary edge is heard in 'Walking On Thin Ice', the Yoko single he helped to complete on the night of his murder.

Paul and Yoko made a public show of reconciliation at the 1994 Hall of Fame ceremony in New York, at which John was inducted as a solo artist.

Roxy Music's version of 'Jealous Guy', recorded just after John's death, was a moving epitaph, catching the universal mood of bittersweet nostalgia. Paul Simon wrote 'The Late Great Johnny Ace', a skilfully constructed elegy to Lennon, that weaves in his demise with those of John F. Kennedy and the original Johnny Ace, an R&B star who shot himself playing Russian roulette in 1954. George Harrison was joined by Paul and Ringo on his own tribute, 'All Those Years Ago'. Yoko's next album, *Season of Glass*, was naturally by way of an ode to John, even re-enlisting Phil Spector for a part of the production. But its cover was hard to take — a photo of John's bloodstained spectacles by a window of the Dakota apartment.

Paul McCartney's personal memorial came in a track on 1982's *Tug of War* album. Called 'Here Today', he describes it as "a song saying, Well, if you were here today you'd probably say what I'm doing is crap. But

The remaining Beatles with their original producer George Martin, publicising 'Free As A Bird' in 1995.

you wouldn't mean it, cos you like me really. It's one of those 'come out from behind your glasses, look at me' kind of things. It was a love song about my relationship with him. I was trying to exorcise the demons in my own head, because it's tough when you have somebody like John slagging you off in public...

"He was a major influence on my life, as I suppose I was on his. But the great thing about me and John was that it was me and John, end of story. Everyone else can say, Well, he did this and so-and-so. But that's the nice thing that I can actually think, when we got in a little room it was me and John who wrote it, not any of these other people who think they all know about it. I was the one in the room with him."

In 1983 Yoko authorised *Heart Play — Unfinished Dialogue*, recordings of the 1980 *Playboy* interviews. After *Milk And Honey*, however, the most essential record released after Lennon's death is *Menlove*

The memorial to John in Strawberry Fields — a section of Central Park, opposite the Dakota, dedicated to his memory.

Avenue. Named after the Liverpool road where John lived with his Aunt Mimi in his later childhood, this 1986 set collects some mid-Seventies outtakes and unused songs. From the Spector *Rock'N'Roll* sessions it has John's and Phil's collaboration, 'Here We Go Again', which is richly dramatic; 'Angel Baby' was a 1960 hit for Rosie & the Originals ("one of my all-time favourite songs," announces John); 'My Baby Left Me' revisits early Elvis, but sluggishly; 'To Know Her Is To Love Her' adapts the old Spector hit. From the *Walls And Bridges* time came John's own song, 'Rock And Roll People', left off the album but given to Johnny Winter, and alternate versions of 'Steel And Glass', 'Scared', 'Old Dirt Road', 'Nobody Loves You (When You're Down And Out)' and 'Bless You'. Shorn of all embellishments, the latter tracks are stark and eerie.

More of John's unreleased songs have appeared on bootlegs, while a wealth of rare material was played in the long-running US radio series *The Lost Lennon Tapes*. Among his most renowned "lost" songs is the scathing 'Serve Yourself', a biting satire on Bob Dylan's 'Gotta Serve Somebody'. In a gutteral Liverpool accent, Lennon ridicules the singer's new religious fervour. (Another of his Dylan skits selected 'Knockin' On Heaven's Door', beginning, "Lord, take this make-up offa me.") In his interviews, though, John was careful not to criticise Dylan's conversion.

There are some rare Lennon tracks scattered around the various "Best Of" sets which have succeeded *Shaved Fish*. The 1982 *John Lennon Collection* found room for another *Walls And Bridges* outtake, 'Move Over Mrs L', a rather throwaway cut which was previously the B-side to 'Stand By Me'. In 1980 there were demo versions of 'Imagine' and the then-unknown 'Real Love' on the documentary soundtrack CD *Imagine: John Lennon*. In 1990 a four-CD box, *Lennon*, included the duets with Elton John at Madison Square Garden. (John's earlier show there, with Elephant's Memory, became a 1986 CD, *Live In New York City*.)

But in 1994 the unthinkable occurred. What nobody had foreseen was that John Lennon's solo legacy would one day be reclaimed by the Beatles. When Paul and Yoko met in New York, to induct John as a solo artist in the Rock & Roll Hall Of Fame, they discussed the unfinished songs that John had written in the Dakota. With the band's *Anthology* films about to be produced, there was a need for musical input from all four members. It was decided that Paul, George and Ringo would take away tapes of 'Real Love' and 'Free As A Bird', both begun around 1977 as part of a projected musical, *The Ballad Of John And Yoko*. In Paul's own studio in Sussex, England, producer Jeff Lynne was summoned to help the band turn John's mono tapes into full recordings.

For the surviving Beatles there were difficulties in the task, both technical and emotional. McCartney recalled, "I said to Ringo, 'Let's pretend that we've nearly finished the recordings and John is just going off to Spain on holiday.' He's rung up saying, 'Look, there's one more song I wouldn't mind getting on the album, it's a good song but it's not finished. Take it in the studio, have fun with it, and I trust you.' And with that scenario in place Ringo said, 'Oh, this could even be joyous!' And it was...

"The good thing about 'Free As A Bird' for us was that it was unfinished. The middle eight didn't have all the words, so that was like John bringing me a song and saying, 'Do you want to finish it?'."

Ringo Starr said of John's absence, "We got over it by feeling that he'd gone for lunch, he'd gone for a cup of tea... It's a sadness because the three of us got pretty close again, and still there's that empty hole, you know, that *is* John... He would have loved being back with us now. A lot of the footage of John is angry, because that's where he was in the Seventies. He was sort of putting the Beatles down. Now he'd have felt differently. He would have loved the new music."

And George added, "Maybe I'm peculiar — but to me he isn't dead. When I never saw him for years before he died, I thought, 'Oh well, he's living in New York and I just haven't seen him in a while.' It's kind of still like that. I don't believe that death is a terminal thing. The soul lives on. We are going to meet again. Life is just shadows, we are shadows on this sunny wall.... I miss John in as much as we could have a good laugh and, also, I think he was a good balance. I miss him in the context of the band because he wouldn't take any shit. I want truth. John was good at that."

'Free As A Bird' and 'Real Love' were each worldwide hits. Further releases from the Lennon vaults cannot be ruled out. Interest in John continues, and is not confined to those who grew up in his time. A generation of musicians, too young to remember the awful news bulletins of December 1980, regards him as their mentor, and strives to capture some of his world-embracing spirit in their own work. Many remember him as the best friend they never had.

As the decades pass, John Lennon's achievements do not fade from our memories. If anything, they seem even more worthwhile. He is undiminished. In the *Imagine* film of 1988, Yoko Ono remembered him this way: "He was my husband, he was my lover, he was my friend, my partner. He was an old soldier that fought with me."

CHRONOLOGY

1940
9 October John Winston Lennon is born in Oxford Street Maternity Hospital, Liverpool.

1946
John's mother Julia has put him in the care of her sister Mimi. His father Freddie offers to take him away to New Zealand, but John decides to stay.

1957
March John forms his first band, the Black Jacks, later named the Quarry Men.
6 July Paul McCartney watches the Quarry Men at a summer fete. He jams with the band and John invites him to join.
September John becomes a student at Liverpool College of Art.

1958
15 July Julia Lennon is killed in a road accident.
Also in this year, the Quarry Men, now including George Harrison, pay to make their first recording, 'That'll Be the Day'.

1960
August Renamed the Beatles, John's group play their first residency in Hamburg.

1962
23 August John marries art school girlfriend Cynthia Powell, who is pregnant with their son Julian.
4 September The Beatles record their first single for EMI, 'Love Me Do'.

1963
29 August The Beatles' single 'She Loves You' tops the UK chart for seven weeks.
4 November The Beatles appear before the Queen at the Royal Command Performance.

1964
9 February Following a riotous welcome in New York, the Beatles play Ed Sullivan's TV show to an audience of 73 million.

1965
15 August The Beatles' first show at Shea Stadium.

1966
4 March John's comment that the Beatles are "now more popular than Jesus" appears in a London paper, stirring bitter controversy in USA.
29 August The Beatles play their last concert, in San Francisco.
9 November John meets Japanese artist Yoko Ono at the Indica Gallery in London.

1967
1 June Release of the Beatles' *Sgt Pepper's Lonely Hearts Club Band.*

1968
20 May In Cynthia's absence, Yoko and John record *Two Virgins* and become lovers.
18 October Police raid the London flat that John has borrowed from Ringo. John pleads guilty to possessing cannabis resin.
21 November Yoko suffers the first in a series of miscarriages.

1969
20 March John and Yoko marry in Gibraltar. After visiting Paris they fly on to Amsterdam, turning their honeymoon into a seven-day "bed-in" for world peace.
22 April John changes his middle name from Winston to Ono.
26 May To Montreal, where a second bed-in produces 'Give Peace a Chance'.
13 September Recording of *Live Peace* in Toronto.
24 October UK release of 'Cold Turkey'.
25 November John returns his MBE to the Queen in an anti-war protest.

1970
27 January John writes and records 'Instant Karma!'.
10 April Paul McCartney announces that the Beatles have disbanded
23 April To Los Angeles for course in Primal Therapy with Dr Arthur Janov.
9 December Release of *John Lennon/Plastic Ono Band.*

1971
22 March US release of 'Power to the People'.
3 September To New York, in search of Yoko's daughter Kyoko. John never returns to UK.
9 September Release of *Imagine.*
1 December US release of 'Happy Xmas (War Is Over)'.

10 December Appearance at the John Sinclair benefit concert in Ann Arbor, Michigan.

1972

16 March John is served with a US deportation order. He lodges an appeal.
19 June Release of *Some Time In New York City*.
30 August Afternoon and evening concerts at Madison Square Garden in support of the One To One children's charity.

1973

1 April At a New York press conference John and Yoko announce the state of Nutopia.
18 September Ringo buys John's English home, Tittenhurst Park.
October John separates from Yoko. With May Pang he leaves for LA and attempts to record an oldies album with Phil Spector.
2 November Release of *Mind Games*.

1974

12 March Drunk and disorderly, John is ejected from the Smothers Brothers show at the Troubadour club.
17 July John is ordered to leave the USA within 60 days. He lodges another appeal.
31 August In the New York federal court, John accuses the Nixon administration of tapping his phone and wishing to deport him for political reasons. His accusations will later be vindicated.
26 September US release of *Walls and Bridges*.
16 November 'Whatever Gets You Thru The Night' becomes John's first solo Number 1 hit in the States.
28 November John keeps a promise by joining Elton John onstage at Madison Square Garden. This will be his last public concert appearance. Yoko and John meet again after the show.

1975

January John returns to live with Yoko at the Dakota in New York. Yoko becomes pregnant.
17 February Release of *Rock'N'Roll* album.
1 March John and Yoko appear together in public at the Grammy awards.
13 June John appears on stage for last time, at the filming of TV special *Salute To Lew Grade*.
9 October On John's 35th birthday, Yoko gives birth to the couple's only son, Sean.

1976

1 April Death of John's father, Freddie Lennon.
27 July Issued with his "Green Card", John is finally granted right of US residency.

1977

20 January John attends inauguration gala of President Jimmy Carter.
4 October John and Yoko hold press conference in Japan, stating their plan to raise Sean before returning to work.

1978

John divides his time between travelling, recording home demo tracks, acting as "househusband", learning Japanese, and writing the autobiographical essay *The Ballad Of John And Yoko*, intended as programme notes for a proposed musical of that name. The essay will later appear in his posthumous book *Skywriting by Word Of Mouth*.

1979

27 May Full page ad, "A love letter from John and Yoko", appears in newspapers around the world.

1980

July John takes a boat trip to Bermuda where he will develop the songs for *Double Fantasy*.
4 August John begins his first studio recordings for five years.
17 November UK release of *Double Fantasy*.
8 December John is shot five times outside the Dakota Building, and dies soon after at the Roosevelt Hospital.

DISCOGRAPHY

All records were released under John Lennon's name except where noted. All songs were written by John except where noted. Most of John's solo records were originally released on the Apple label. Reissues and CDs have generally been on EMI or Parlophone in the UK, Capitol in the US.

1. SINGLES

These were the only songs issued as singles in their own right, and written for that purpose rather than as album tracks. The A-sides can now be found on various compilation albums. 'Free as a Bird' and 'Real Love' appear on Volumes I and II, respectively, of the *Beatles' Anthology.*

(PLASTIC ONO BAND)
'Give Peace A Chance' (Lennon/ McCartney)/ 'Remember Love' (Yoko)
UK: 4 July 1969
US: 7 July 1969
APPLE

(PLASTIC ONO BAND)
'Cold Turkey'/ 'Don't Worry Kyoko' (Yoko)
UK: 24 October 1969
US: 20 October 1969
APPLE

'Instant Karma!'/ 'Who Has Seen The Wind?' (Yoko)
UK: 6 February 1970
US: 20 February 1970
APPLE

'Power To The People'/ 'Open Your Box' (Yoko) (This track was later retitled 'Hirake'; in the US it was replaced by another Yoko song, 'Touch Me')
UK: 12 March 1971
US: 22 March 1971
APPLE

'Happy Xmas (War Is Over)' (with Yoko)/ 'Listen, The Snow Is Falling' (Yoko)
UK: 24 November 1972
US: 1 December 1971
APPLE

2. ALBUMS

(JOHN LENNON & YOKO ONO)
Unfinished Music No. 1 — Two Virgins 'Two Virgins 1-10'; 'Together'; 'Hushabye Hushabye'.
UK: 29 November 1968
US: 11 November 1968
APPLE/TETRAGRAMMATON

(JOHN LENNON & YOKO ONO)
Unfinished Music No. 2 — Life with the Lions
'Cambridge 1969'; 'No Bed For Beatle John'; 'Baby's Heartbeat'; 'Two Minutes Of Silence'; 'Radio Play'.
UK: 9 May 1969
US: 26 May 1969
ZAPPLE

(JOHN LENNON & YOKO ONO)
Wedding Album
'John And Yoko'; 'Amsterdam'.
UK: 7 November 1969
US: 20 October 1969
APPLE

(THE PLASTIC ONO BAND)
Live Peace in Toronto
'Blue Suede Shoes' (Perkins); 'Money' (Bradford/Gordy); 'Dizzy Miss Lizzy' (Williams); 'Yer Blues' (Lennon/ McCartney); 'Cold Turkey'; 'Give Peace A Chance' (Lennon/ McCartney); 'Don't Worry Kyoko (Mummy's Only Looking For Her Hand In The Snow)' (Yoko); 'John, John (Let's Hope For Peace)' (Yoko).
UK and US: 12 December 1969
APPLE

John Lennon/Plastic Ono Band
'Mother'; 'Hold On'; 'I Found Out'; 'Working Class Hero'; 'Isolation'; 'Remember'; 'Love'; 'Well Well Well'; 'Look At Me'; 'God'; 'My Mummy's Dead'.
UK and US: 11 December 1970
APPLE

Imagine
'Imagine'; 'Crippled Inside'; 'Jealous Guy'; 'It's So Hard'; 'I Don't Want To Be A Soldier'; 'Gimme Some Truth'; 'Oh My Love' (with Yoko); 'How Do You Sleep?'; 'How?'; 'Oh Yoko!'.
UK: 8 October 1971
US: 9 September 1971
APPLE

(JOHN & YOKO/ PLASTIC ONO BAND)
Some Time in New York City
'Woman Is The Nigger Of The World' (with Yoko); 'Sisters O Sisters (Yoko); 'Attica State' (with Yoko); 'Born In A Prison' (Yoko); 'New York City'; 'Sunday Bloody Sunday' (with Yoko); 'The Luck Of The Irish' (with Yoko); 'John Sinclair'; 'Angela' (with Yoko); 'We're All Water' (Yoko); 'Cold Turkey'; 'Don't Worry Kyoko' (Yoko); 'Well (Baby Please Don't Go)' (Walter Ward); 'Jamrag' (with Yoko); 'Scumbag' (with Yoko and Frank Zappa); 'Au' (with Yoko).
UK: 15 September 1972
US: 12 June 1972
APPLE

Mind Games
'Mind Games'; 'Tight A$'; 'Aisumasen (I'm Sorry)'; 'One Day (At A Time)'; 'Bring On The Lucie (Freda Peeple)'; 'Nutopian International Anthem'; 'Intuition'; 'Out The Blue'; 'Only People'; 'I Know (I Know)'; 'You Are Here'; 'Meat City'.
UK: 16 November 1973
US: 2 November 1973
APPLE

Walls and Bridges
'Going Down On Love'; 'Whatever Gets You Thru The Night'; 'Old Dirt Road' (with Harry Nilsson); 'What You Got'; 'Bless You'; 'Scared'; '#9 Dream'; 'Surprise Surprise (Sweet Bird Of Paradox)'; 'Steel And Glass'; 'Beef Jerky'; 'Nobody Loves You (When You're Down And Out)'; 'Ya Ya' (Robinson/Dorsey/Lewis).
UK: 4 October 1974
US: 26 September 1974
APPLE

Rock'n'Roll
'Be-Bop-a-Lula' (Davis/Vincent); 'Stand By Me' (King/Leiber/ Stoller); 'Rip It Up (Blackwell/ Marascalco); 'Ready Teddy' (Blackwell/

Marascalco); 'You Can't Catch Me' (Berry); 'Ain't That A Shame' (Domino/ Batholomew); 'Do You Want To Dance' (Freeman); 'Sweet Little Sixteen' (Berry); 'Slippin' And Slidin' (Penniman/ Bocage/Collins/Smith); 'Peggy Sue' (Holly/ Allison/Petty); 'Bring It On Home To Me' (Cooke); 'Send Me Some Lovin' (Price/ Marascalco); 'Bony Moronie' (Williams); 'Ya Ya' (Robinson/Dorsey/ Lewis); 'Just Because' (Price).
UK: 21 February 1975
US: 17 February 1975
APPLE

(JOHN LENNON & YOKO ONO)
Double Fantasy
'(Just Like) Starting Over'; 'Kiss Kiss Kiss' (Yoko); 'Cleanup Time'; 'Give Me Something' (Yoko); 'I'm Losing You'; 'I'm Moving On' (Yoko); 'Beautiful Boy (Darling Boy)'; 'Watching The Wheels'; 'I'm Your Angel' (Yoko); 'Woman'; 'Beautiful Boys' (Yoko); 'Dear Yoko'; 'Every Man Has A Woman Who Loves Him' (Yoko); 'Hard Times Are Over' (Yoko).
UK and US: 17 November 1980
GEFFEN

(JOHN LENNON & YOKO ONO)
Milk and Honey
'I'm Stepping Out'; 'Sleepless Night'; 'I Don't Wanna Face It'; 'Don't Be Scared'; 'Nobody Told Me'; 'O'Sanity'; 'Borrowed Time'; 'Your Hands'; '(Forgive Me) My Little Flower Princess'; 'Let Me Count the Ways'; 'Grow Old With Me'; 'You're The One'. (All songs co-credited to Yoko)
UK: 23 January 1984
US: 19 January 1984
POLYDOR

Live in New York City
'New York City'; 'It's So Hard'; Woman Is The Nigger Of The World' (with Yoko); 'Well Well Well'; 'Instant Karma!'; 'Mother'; 'Come Together' (Lennon/ McCartney); 'Imagine'; 'Cold Turkey'; 'Hound Dog' (Leiber/Stoller); 'Give Peace A Chance' (Lennon/McCartney).
UK and US: 24 January 1986
EMI (UK)/CAPITOL (US)

Menlove Avenue
'Here We Go Again' (with Phil Spector); 'Rock And Roll People'; 'Angel Baby' (Hamlin); 'Since My Baby Left Me' (Pending); 'To Know Her Is To Love Her' (Spector); 'Steel And Glass'; 'Scared'; 'Old Dirt Road' (with Harry Nilsson); 'Nobody Loves You (When You're Down And Out)'; 'Bless You'.
UK: 3 November 1986
US: 27 October 1986
PARLOPHONE (UK)/CAPITOL (US)

3. COMPILATIONS

Shaved Fish
'Give Peace A Chance' (Lennon/ McCartney); 'Cold Turkey'; 'Instant Karma!'; 'Power To The People'; 'Mother'; 'Woman Is The Nigger Of The World' (with Yoko); 'Imagine'; 'Whatever Gets You Thru The Night'; 'Mind Games'; '#9 Dream'; 'Reprise: Give Peace A Chance'.
UK and US: 24 October 1975
APPLE

The John Lennon Collection
'Give Peace A Chance' (Lennon/ McCartney); 'Instant Karma!'; 'Power To The People'; 'Whatever Gets You Thru The Night'; '#9 Dream'; 'Mind Games'; 'Love'; 'Imagine'; 'Jealous Guy'; '(Just Like) Starting Over'; 'Woman'; 'I'm Losing You'; 'Beautiful Boy (Darling Boy)'; 'Dear Yoko'; 'Watching The Wheels'; 'Cold Turkey'; 'Move Over Mrs L'; 'Happy Xmas (War Is Over)' (with Yoko) (UK only); 'Stand By Me' (King/Leiber/Stoller) (UK only).
UK: 23 October 1989 (replaced a 1982 Geffen version)
US: 19 February 1990 (replaced a 1982 Geffen version)
EMI (UK)/CAPITOL (US)

Imagine: John Lennon
'Real Love' (demo version); 'Imagine' (studio and demo versions); 'Give Peace A Chance' (Lennon/ McCartney); 'How?'; 'God'; 'Mother' (live version); 'Stand By Me' (King/Leiber/Stoller); 'Jealous Guy'; 'Woman'; 'Beautiful Boy (Darling Boy)'; '(Just Like) Starting Over'. Also the following Beatle tracks: 'Twist And Shout'; 'Help!'; 'In My Life'; 'Strawberry Fields Forever'; 'A Day In The Life'; 'Revolution 1'; 'The Ballad Of John And Yoko'; 'Julia'; 'Don't Let Me Down'.
UK: 10 October 1988
US: 4 October 1988
PARLOPHONE (UK)/CAPITOL (US)

Lennon
'Give Peace A Chance' (Lennon/ McCartney); 'Blue Suede Shoes' (Perkins); 'Money' (Bradford/Gordy); 'Dizzy Miss Lizzy' (Williams); 'Yer Blues' (Lennon/ McCartney); 'Cold Turkey'; 'Instant Karma!'; 'Mother'; 'Hold On'; 'I Found Out'; 'Working Class Hero'; 'Isolation'; 'Remember'; 'Love'; 'Well Well Well'; 'Look At Me'; 'God'; 'My Mummy's Dead'; 'Well (Baby Please Don't Go)' (Walter Ward); 'Imagine'; 'Crippled Inside'; 'Jealous Guy'; 'It's So Hard'; 'Gimme Some Truth'; 'Oh My Love' (with Yoko); 'How Do You Sleep?'; 'How?'; 'Oh Yoko!'; 'Happy Xmas (War Is Over)' (with Yoko); 'Woman Is the Nigger Of The World' (with Yoko); 'New York City'; 'John Sinclair'; 'Come Together' (Lennon/McCartney); 'Hound Dog' (Leiber/ Stoller)'; 'Mind Games'; 'Aisumasen (I'm Sorry)'; 'One Day (At A Time)'; 'Intuition'; 'Out The Blue'; 'Whatever Gets You Thru The Night'; 'Going Down On Love'; 'Old Dirt Road (with Harry Nilsson); 'Bless You'; 'Scared'; '#9 Dream'; 'Surprise Surprise (Sweet Bird Of Paradox)'; 'Steel And Glass'; 'Nobody Loves You (When You're Down And Out)'; 'Stand By Me' (King/ Leiber/Stoller); 'Ain't That A Shame' (Domino/ Batholomew); 'Do You Want to Dance' (Freeman); 'Sweet Little Sixteen' (Berry); 'Slippin And Slidin' (Penniman/ Bocage/Collins/Smith); 'Angel Baby' (Hamlin); 'Just Because' (Price); 'Whatever Gets You Thru The Night' (live with Elton John); 'Lucy In The Sky With Diamonds' (Lennon/McCartney) (live with Elton John); 'I Saw Her Standing There' (Lennon/McCartney) (live with Elton John); '(Just Like) Starting Over'; 'Cleanup Time'; 'I'm Losing You'; 'Beautiful Boy (Darling Boy)'; 'Watching The Wheels'; 'Woman'; 'Dear Yoko'; 'I'm Stepping Out' (with Yoko); 'I Don't Wanna Face It' (with Yoko); 'Nobody Told Me' (with Yoko); 'Borrowed Time' (with Yoko); '(Forgive Me) My Little Flower Princess' (with Yoko); 'Every Man Has A Woman Who Loves Him' (Yoko); 'Grow Old With Me' (with Yoko).
UK and US: 30 October 1990
EMI (UK)/CAPITOL (US)

INDEX

Numbers in italic refer to illustrations